What people are saying about ...

Act Two

"Order takeout, kick off your shoes, and turn off your phone: Kimberly Stuart delivers another sassy, funny novel with a high-strung heroine you'll love! Get ready to curl up with a laugh-out-loud book!"

Ginger Garrett, author of *Chosen*
and *In the Shadow of Lions*

"Like fine music, fine novels entertain us with tempo, depth, and well-timed crescendos. In *Act Two*, Kimberly Stuart proves herself a deft composer. Bravo!"

Ray Blackston, author of *Flabbergasted*

"From the shimmering streets of Manhattan to the snow-covered fields of Iowa, *Act Two* delivers an entertaining and redeeming story about the power of second chances. Bravo!"

Anne Dayton and May Vanderbilt,
authors of *The Book of Jane*

"*Act Two* is not just a novel in perfect pitch, there's a joyful grace note calling us to God on every page. Kim Stuart's most fun and stirring novel yet."

Claudia Mair Burney, author of
Zora and Nicky and *Wounded*

Act Two

ACT TWO

A Novel in Perfect Pitch

By

Kimberly Stuart

David C Cook®

transforming lives together

ACT TWO
Published by David C. Cook
4050 Lee Vance View
Colorado Springs, CO 80918 U.S.A.

David C. Cook Distribution Canada
55 Woodslee Avenue, Paris, Ontario, Canada N3L 3E5

David C. Cook U.K., Kingsway Communications
Eastbourne, East Sussex BN23 6NT, England

David C. Cook and the graphic circle C logo
are registered trademarks of Cook Communications Ministries.

This story is a work of fiction. All characters and events are
the product of the author's imagination. Any resemblance
to any person, living or dead, is coincidental.

All Scripture reference taken from the *Holy Bible,
New International Version*®. *NIV*®. Copyright © 1973,
1978, 1984 by International Bible Society. Used by
permission of Zondervan. All rights reserved.

LCCN 2008922802
Mass market ISBN 978-1-4347-6441-6

© 2008 Kimberly Stuart
The author is represented by MacGregor Literary

The Team: Andrea Christian, Jamie Chavez,
Jaci Schneider, Karen Athen and Sarah Schultz
Cover Design: The DesignWorks Group, Tim Green
Interior Design: The DesignWorks Group

Printed in the United States of America
First Edition 2008

1 2 3 4 5 6 7 8 9 10

022608

To my dad and my grandpas,
real Iowa "farm boys" and
men after God's own heart.

Acknowledgments

If it weren't for the following people, this book would certainly not be in your hands right now and I, its humble author, would still be padding around my house in slippers and pajamas, bereft of good hygiene and full of ideas that never saw the outside of my crazy head. So I, my husband, my children, my neighbors, and our postman would like to thank, in no particular order:

My parents for teaching me how to love life and laugh at it too.

Ryan, Jen, Lindsay, Jimmy, and Scott for believing I can (or at least not doubting out loud).

The Roggen, Ruisch, and Welge families, for their tenacious love.

Ryan, Bets, Livi, and Jonah, for friendship across the decades. Welcome, Jonah. We love you.

Todd Swanson, who made me sound far more sophisticated than I am. He deserves a cut of the royalties but is, unfortunately, disqualified as all hedge fund managers must be.

Wade Foster, for his unfailing, long-beloved friendship and sweet connections in the theater world. You defy gravity, my dear.

Suzanne Ohlmann, for all the inexplicables and for knowing everything about everything.

Kristen, Amy H., and Amy D., for their exemplary work as moms and friends and for still laughing at my jokes.

Sandra, David, Hannah, and Colin McDill, for their courage. Sandi and Loretta, you are my most precious pork queens. I owe you.

All the book clubs, library peeps, women's groups, and readers the world over who share their thoughts with me. A special blessing to Julie David and her Read-It-And-Reapers for letting me speak inappropriately and loving me anyway.

The pros: Andrea Christian, Terry Behimer, Jaci Schneider, Kate Amaya, Ingrid Beck, and the whole team at David C. Cook. Please don't realize what a great deal I'm getting. I've never been fired before.

Jamie Chavez, for pushing and prodding and inspiring and chortling, all at the best times. Any room on your new shelves for this one?

Independent bookstores like Beaverdale Books, the

Book Vault, East Village Books, and Hill Avenue Book Company, for carrying my novels and recommending them to readers. Gems, all of you.

Writers' group smarties Jen, Wendy, Mia, Dawn, and Kali, for their work on this manuscript and for loving the written word as much as I.

Dr. Gary and Barb Rosberg, for championing marriage and offering their friendship.

Tara Bakken, for pressing on with courage and grace.

The amazing Chip MacGregor, who is brilliant, funny, and one of my favorite gifts from God.

Thank you, Marc, Ani, and Mitch, for your sweetness in the face of all my salt, your generosity of spirit even when I'm feeling stingy, and your willingness to walk closely beside me, mile after mile, word by word. I love you so much it hurts.

And thank You, Jesus. You know my heart.

I

Relic

I once had a therapist who blamed my dislike of children on the Korean War. I was never entirely sure how she made that connection. Something to do with my father's inability to serve because of bunions. Or maybe it was my much-analyzed only-child complex. At any rate, she left private practice to become a consultant for *Montel,* and I was left with my visceral distaste for Baby Gap and Shirley Temple healthy and intact.

Children unnerved me. They moved like their internal remote was stuck on fast-forward. I never knew how to protect myself. That particular winter morning, for example, I was tempted to think the little girl with a velvet ribbon in her hair was benign, cherubic, even. And the next thing I knew, she reached over to wipe a cocoa-sopped little mitt on my new Burberry skirt.

"Not so fast, young lady," I said to the criminal as I put out my hand to stop hers. I took a step back and locked eyes with the girl. She looked to be about five. I cleared my throat and enunciated like I was in diction class, working to be heard above the throng in Tasia's Coffee Shop. "Your mommy is nearly finished paying."

Mommy half turned, keeping her palm open above the counter to catch her change. Her cheeks were flushed and her eyes flickered like those who have been subjected to endless hours of child-adult interaction. "Francesca," she said to the girl, who stared at me with doe eyes. Francesca was still holding her wet hand in front of her and letting cocoa drip onto Tasia's floor.

"Can I help you?" A teenager with a pierced lip slouched behind the register and looked at me.

"You may," I said and rattled off my usual. "Large decaf soy white chocolate mocha. Light on the chocolate with a sprinkle of nutmeg." I edged around Francesca in a careful arc and set my mahogany leather clutch on the countertop. "Extra hot." I watched the barista move rapid-fire to concoct my drink. My eyes stayed trained on my cup, as my request for nutmeg had been ignored in times past.

"Sorry to bother you." Mommy poked her head around and invaded my personal space. Must have been genetic.

"No harm done," I said without looking up from my purse. I handed the cashier a crisp ten. "There are extra napkins near the door."

She kept staring until I turned to face her. "It *is* you!" she exclaimed. Her voice was nasal and high. "I can't believe it. You're Sadie Maddox, right?"

I dropped the paltry change from my ten into my clutch. After a careful sip of my mocha, I moved to make room for the next customer. Mommy followed me with a bouncing Francesca close behind. "I am," I said with a slow nod. I smiled before taking another sip.

"My mother is not going to believe this," the woman said. "She used to play your records for me when I was in junior high. We'd try to sing along with the Italian, which never went too well, but I really feel all that foreign language stuff gave me an appreciation for high culture, you know?" The woman wore a jaunty red beret, which did not quite contain a head of light blonde curls. The timbre of her voice could have caused epileptic seizures; I realized I was squinting in some kind of misguided self-defense. Nevertheless, she did appear to be earnest.

"I appreciate your kind words," I said. "Give your mother my regards." I meant this as a parting gesture but she stayed.

"There was this one song I just loved. I can't remember the name but it went like this." She started in with a hum that cut through the buzz of Tasia's noon rush. This woman was nothing less than remarkable.

I remained silent, as I most certainly did not recognize the melody through that narrow nasal passage. I shot a glance around the room for Avi but saw no sign of him.

"Remember?" the woman asked. She was a tenacious, humming bulldog. "It always reminded me of the beginning of 'Let's Get Physical' by Olivia Newton-John."

All right. "Yes, well, it's been a pleasure to meet you and best wishes for a happy holiday." I tried moving to the side but was startled when little Francesca jumped out and roared.

"Sorry," Mommy said with a little laugh.

I clutched my heart.

"She's really into roaring. We saw *Lion King* on Broadway a few months ago. Franny loves music, don't you, sweetie?"

Franny roared again, this time showing me her fangs.

"Is that right?" I said, waving to Avi, who had just entered. He was shaking the snow from his coat and didn't see me. "Francesca, do you like Italian art song like the other women in your family?"

Mommy shook her curls. "Oh, no. We don't even have a record player any more. She's more into Disney." She stopped her yammering and cleared her throat. "But we really should buy more classical CDs. I've been meaning to get around to that." She looked embarrassed and busied herself combing her fingers through Francesca's mop of hair. The child stared at me and stuck out her tongue when Mommy wasn't looking.

"Yes, well. You'll excuse me," I said, nodding to the two of them and eking out a tight smile before escaping with my mocha to a table by the window.

♪

So now you know. I'm famous. It seems indelicate to say it that way, but we might as well be out with it. I am an artist, a singer to be more precise. I trained at two of the most prestigious conservatories in this country, did a widely coveted apprenticeship with a European opera legend, and spent a decade being flown around the world to sing all the major roles for a mezzo-soprano. The incident with scary little Francesca and her mother still played out several times a month, though most times without the humming, for which we could all be grateful. To be recognized in a city like New York was a coup. I saw it as a barometer of sorts to gauge if I was still a presence in the fickle music world.

Visibility is everything, my agent always said, and would likely say again when he returned to our table with his cappuccino. I smirked into my steaming mug. Visibility offered only so many choices to a woman who'd just turned forty. Couldn't be flashing my groceries to the paparazzi, for example. Sordid love affairs weren't as titillating when the flesh factor sagged more than it sweated. One had to be crafty at this age and combine class with sass.

I straightened in my chair, newly pleased that I'd called this meeting with Avi. If anyone was capable of helping me map out a plan, it had to be Avi Feldman, that shark of a New York agent who signed a new client only if six-figure fees were involved. I bit the inside of my cheek, freshly chagrined at the exorbitant percentage the man skimmed from each of my paychecks. The price would pay off, I assured myself, flashing my new veneers at him across the room. Didn't one have to spend money to make money? Avi would know how to engage the likes of fanged Franny and her beret-sporting mother.

Record player, indeed.

♪

"Happy Hanukkah," I said and leaned over to peck him on the cheek.

"Thanks," Avi said around his return kiss. "And Merry Exploitation of Your Own Messiah." He smirked while unwrapping himself from a charcoal leather coat and silk scarf. "You Christians do have a way with pagan holidays."

"Watch it or we'll get a hold of Yom Kippur and start selling Day of Atonement cell phone accessories."

"Appalling," he said and turned to face me. "You look fantastic," he said by way of professional appraisal. "Did you get your eyes lifted?"

"Thank you, and no," I said, pleased and huffy at the same time. "Not all women over forty resort to the scalpel."

He snorted into his doll-sized cappuccino mug. "Since when are you so well-adjusted?"

I took a deep breath, exhaled slowly. "I'm embracing the fullness of age."

Avi raised one eyebrow. I suspected he waxed. "Yes, about that." He tipped back his cup to drain it. "How are you feeling about your audience turnout lately?"

I felt my eyes widening. "I feel fine. Positive, I should say. The recital at St. Mark's—" The show hadn't sold out, but then I'd agreed to do it as a favor to an old friend. "We were—what—three-quarters full?"

"Half."

"Half. Well." I smoothed my hair. "Respectable, anyway, particularly so close to the holidays."

"Sadie, I think you should try something new. Think total departure, breathing new life into old ideas, well-worn songs, familiar repertoire."

"Yes," I said, nodding vigorously. I put one hand over his and couldn't help but notice my manicure was stunning. "I'm *so* pleased you're saying this, Avi, because I've been giving this issue a lot of thought. I think I need a late-career reinvention of sorts."

"Exactly."

"Because I'm not that Lindy Lohan girl."

"Lindsay."

"Yes, of course. I'm not twenty but I think I'm *better* than I was at twenty. I'm wiser, more comfortable in my own skin, better able to choose what suits my voice." I paused, tilting my head in thought and breathing in Tasia's intoxicating aroma of cinnamon, cloves and caffeine. After allowing a moment to bask in the magnitude of female maturity, I returned my gaze to his face. "I'm *more*, Avi."

"Well," he said, leaning back in his chair and opening his arms. "You'll be pleased to know I have the perfect opportunity for you and your fuller, wiser, better self."

I cupped both hands around the waning warmth in my mug. "I'm open to absolutely everything. What's our next adventure?" I winked as I took a last sip of my mocha.

"Visiting professor of voice at a small liberal arts college." Avi waited for my reaction.

My sip became a pull even though the last dregs of drink had gone cold. "Professor of voice. I see. I don't have a PhD."

"They couldn't care less. You're Sadie Maddox."

True enough. "Would I have to teach classes or just have a studio of students?"

"Negotiable."

I tapped one finger on the porcelain saucer and took a moment to think. My eyes drifted around the room. Tasia's was decked out for everybody's holiday. Lit wreaths hung in each of the five tall café windows in front, silver menorahs lined a glass shelf behind the counter, and Kwanzaa candles were for sale by the register. I loved New York.

Avi cleared his throat. "And the best part is that you'll be able to escape the craziness of urban life."

I snapped my eyes back to his. "Why on earth would I want to do that?"

"Because the college is in Iowa."

I paused and then burst into schoolgirl laughter. "Avi, come on. Tell me where this school really is. Which borough? Brooklyn? Queens? I'll even go to Long Island in a pinch." My smile was conciliatory.

Avi took both of my hands in his, leaned forward, and kissed one cheek. "Sadie," he whispered. He kissed the other cheek and whispered in my other ear. "Iowa." He kept his cheek on mine, likely to discourage a dramatic response.

I pushed him away and shrieked, "Are you insane?" People turned in their seats but I ignored them. People staring at me was nothing new. "What, in the name of all that is good, is in Iowa? Corn? Cows? Wal-Mart?"

"Honey," Avi said in the voice of a therapist. He made his living working with hysterical people. "I can understand your reluctance. I've seen *Music Man* and *Field of Dreams*. But you just told me you need a fresh direction, am I right?"

"Fresh does *not* mean mind-numbing, culture-barren, provincial—*need* I go on?"

Avi took a manila envelope out of his satchel. "Take a look at the particulars," he said, handing it to me. "Even without subletting your apartment, this is a financial no-brainer. You'll have a break from the recital circuit, you can cultivate fans in a different part of the country—"

"You mean all twenty-four of the people who live there."

"—and you can try your hand at teaching. It might just be the perfect fit."

I'd come to this meeting thinking a Gap ad, a spot on *Martha Stewart,* at the very least a cover story in *Good Housekeeping* or something equally maternal. And Avi was suggesting Iowa. Things must have been worse than I thought.

"How are CD sales?" I asked, shoulders slumped.

Avi cleared his throat. "Not very good. And your performance calendar is nearly empty for the spring." He looked at his watch and stood. "Listen, love, just think about it. Look over the materials, consult with all the smart people you know, and you'll end up admitting I'm right on this. One semester. That's it. They're in a time crunch, they'll fork out the cash, and you could use it. It's not Carnegie, but you said yourself that hall is overrated anyway." He leaned down to kiss the top of my head. "Call me."

He walked away, leaving me to wallow in a stack of glossy brochures with photographs of people with bad hair. So things *were* worse than I'd feared. Not only was I getting old, losing audiences, and selling fewer CDs, I was a prime candidate for midwest living.

Merry blasted Christmas.

2

West Nineties

Later that afternoon, I dragged my tired feet back uptown after five hours of shopping and errand running. The wind had picked up to the point of being ridiculous, and I found it impossible to be pleasant. When I reached Jasmine, my neighborhood Indian restaurant, I gritted my teeth and pulled the door open against a gust of arctic air. The door slammed behind me, letting loose a peal from a cluster of tiny bells hanging above.

Atreya, the gentleman who ran Jasmine with his wife, Pakshi, hustled from the back of the restaurant. His face lit up when he saw me. "Miss Sadie, welcome. You look, *ehm*, rather cold. Would you like some tea?" His brow creased in worry to see my face unchanged from its horror of the outside.

"Atreya," I said, "rest assured I am *trying* to smile at you. My face is still thawing."

"Yes, yes, of course," he said, leading me by the elbow to sit down at a nearby table. "Pakshi is finishing your order. Please, sit and relax. Please."

I nodded. "Here," I said. I rummaged through my purse and extracted the nearest credit card. "Twenty percent gratuity."

"Thank you, Miss Sadie," Atreya said, and left me for the cash register.

After twenty years of living in New York, one would think I'd have been better acclimated to harsh winters. One would be wrong. The wind, the sleet, the snow, the cold—I had nothing redemptive to say about any of it. At least in other parts of the country winter had a purpose. Didn't farmers, for instance, want things to freeze? Something about the death of all living things, circle of life, Elton John, and such. But what, exactly, were we presuming to water in New York City? Concrete? Steel? One good sprinkler system would take care of the whole of Central Park, our only formidable green space. Harsh winters were nothing but archaic in the urban jungle and yet they continued to visit with all their ferocity and bad manners. And so by mid-December each year, I became an embittered woman who could not be cheered even by good cashmere.

"Miss Sadie," Atreya said when he returned carrying a large paper bag. "You will find the *naan* still hot from the oven and extra slices of lemon for the chicken *tikka masala*."

"You indulge me, Atreya," I said, feeling steam rise to my face from an opening in the top of the bag. "You tell Pakshi that she makes the best Indian food in all of Manhattan."

Atreya grinned and patted my gloved hand. "I will tell her, thank you. Take care in this weather, Miss Sadie." He peered into my face. "It is not for the weak-hearted."

"That, my friend, is the problem," I said and closed my eyes to prepare for reentry to the tundra.

My apartment building was only a block and a half away, but I cursed the distance anyway. *Should have called for delivery*, I thought as Bach's Fugue in C Minor began to play deep within the pocket of my wool coat. My pace slowed to a shuffle, and I tried to extract the phone without dropping my dinner. Just before voice mail swooped in to rescue my caller from a tiresome fourth ring, I flipped open the phone and yelled, "Hello?"

"Have mercy, woman, must you shout?"

"Richard," I said. "We're having gale-force winds. Can you hear me?"

"Darling, all of Long Island can hear you."

"I'm almost home," I said, crossing the street during a yellow light and ignoring the honking horns that accompanied my passage. Civility was dead.

"Why are you out if the weather is so miserable? Doesn't sound like you," Richard said. He would know, as he used to be my husband, long, long ago, when George the First and Barbara had just moved into the White House, and Richard and I were mere children.

"Richard, hold on one moment," I said and pulled the phone away from my ear. "Thank you, Tom," I said to the champion doorman who'd spotted my labored approach and had come to give me a hand.

"You're welcome, Ms. Maddox," Tom said, taking the bag of food and giving me his arm. His eyes were deep brown and framed in a quilt of dark curled lashes. Tom was new in the building and couldn't have been more than twenty-one. He treated me like I was his cherished mother. Mathematically possible, perhaps, but I tried not to dwell on it.

"Call me Sadie," I said when we'd reached the foyer and the door closed behind us. "How many times must we go over this, Tom?"

"I'm a slow study, Ms. Maddox," Tom said, his impossibly white teeth exposed by a charmer of a smile. "Should I help you upstairs?"

I took the bag from him. "Of course not," I said, one eyebrow raised. "I may have just had a milestone birthday, Tommy, but I *am* still mobile. You're welcome to tag along, though, if you're in the mood for Jasmine."

"I've eaten, thank you." His eyes shone. I wondered if he treated all his female residents to the same schoolboy grin or he granted it now because we were drawing near to the Christmas tipping season.

He held the elevator door for me and I slipped in. "Enjoy your evening," he said.

"You too," I said, and we smiled at each other as the door closed.

I was still smiling as the elevator passed the third floor and I heard squawking from my open phone. "Richard?"

I said, but I was too late and the call dropped into a wireless abyss.

I stepped out onto the twelfth floor and opened 1218, my one-bedroom flat with views of the Hudson. Richard and I rented this place together fifteen years ago, heady with a new marriage and his first substantial paycheck. At final count, though, Richard and I were married for only six months. Enough to horrify our parents, throw a few dishes at each other, and realize we'd made a serious mistake. No children to suffer, not even a dog, and the marriage was over. Call it premonition or good sense, but I'd even kept the gift receipt for our toaster.

I hung my coat on an exquisite brushed-platinum coat rack that stood at attention in the foyer, a gift from a wealthy opera patron during my first run of *La Traviata*. Not yet five o'clock and my home was filled with the hurried lavender of descending dusk. I reached to turn on floor lamps on the way to my bedroom, where I dropped my load of packages on the wrought-iron queen bed. If the *tikka* hadn't been waiting for me, I would have considered accepting the polite invitation from my down comforter and taking an early evening nap.

Bach again. I hurried back to the foyer and retrieved my phone before it vibrated off the entry table.

"Richard."

"You have lousy phone etiquette."

"I'm sorry. I lost reception in the elevator."

"Actually, I think you checked out on me sometime around this comment." Richard cleared his throat and willed his voice to a high falsetto. "'Oh, Tommy dear, do call me *Sadie*.'"

"What a horrible impersonation."

"Tom a real dish, then?"

I scooped a pile of steaming basmati onto a plate and drenched the rice with Pakshi's magic. "I have shoes older than Tom." My first bite was glorious. I closed my eyes in gratitude for women who'd done as their mothers told them and learned to cook.

Richard cackled into the phone, very much disturbing my bliss. "You most certainly do not, Sadie Maddox. I've seen your closet. I divorced you over your closet."

I sprinkled drops of lemon juice onto my dinner. "Richard, I know truthfulness is a stretch for you, but let's give it a whirl. Are you trying to imply that, after all these years you (a) are jealous of another man in my life, (b) have become circumspect about our divorce, and/or (c) think I am the only one with a clothes issue?"

He laughed and I smiled. "Touché, my dear, touché. Tell me how you are."

The teapot I'd put on to a high boil started a wild crescendo. I poured myself a cup and sat down to my dinner once more. "I met with Avi today. Turns out Sadie Maddox is a has-been."

"Pshaw," Richard said. I could imagine his eyes rolling toward his salt-and-pepper hairline. "Fire him. He charges too much anyway. Call Judith. I've been telling you this for years."

I met Richard when we were both students at the conservatory, he a doctoral student in orchestral conducting and I beginning my undergrad studies in vocal performance. Richard was everything my sweet Lutheran mother had warned me against: charming, flirtatious, professionally driven, and perpetually single. Our brief marriage cured none of these ills.

"Avi is not the problem, Richard. I am the problem. Or maybe society as a whole. Mature women in our culture are not valued, at least not for their entertainment quotient." I patted my mouth with a napkin. "Too many nubile young things, dewy fresh and trembling from their Met debuts."

Richard let out something of a whinny. The drama quotient between the two of us was no small part of our demise. "For shame, Sadie Maddox! Do not give in to them! Think of Meryl! Think of Helen Mirren! Renée Fleming, for God's sake. She's certainly no spring chicken."

"Well," I said and tossed back the rest of my tea. I slammed the cup down on my granite countertop. "Apparently the world of performing arts has its quota of older women and the quota has been reached."

"I don't believe it for a minute."

"Ahem," I said. "Are you saying your own proclivity for the younger among us has experienced some sort of evolution?" Richard, though a man with many strengths, never got over his weakness for perk. Now in his early fifties, his last girlfriend was named Muffy, a sculpted and bronzed personal trainer who was "really into" older men.

"I am currently single, though I don't see what that has to do with anything."

I sighed. "Avi thinks I should move to Iowa." I heard something drop and Richard cursed. "Richard? Are you all right?"

"Bloody … Dreadful thing … Yes, yes, I'm fine. I was merely startled by your last comment, which I surely fabricated in my twisted, aging mind. Tell me you didn't say Iowa."

"I did." I rose from my chair at the breakfast bar. My kitchen was small but functional. Its most promising feature was that it opened up to the main living space and shared the view offered by a picture window on the south wall. I leaned against the counter and stared at the confetti of lights spreading across the darkened city. "Teaching voice at Moravia College in Maplewood." I recited the info I'd gleaned from my quick read in Tasia's. "Apparently the school itself is very well regarded. Liberal arts, small student-faculty ratio, respectable numbers of Fulbrights and Rhodes. And the music program isn't bad, either."

Richard snorted. "Never heard of it."

"And so you assume it's worthless." I poured another cup of tea and moved toward the couch. "Don't you think that's a bit egocentric?"

"Whoa, whoa, whoa. Why so defensive? Are you actually considering doing this?"

"No, of course not." I deflated into the couch cushions. Italian black leather, by the way. "Maybe. No. I'm just tired and feeling unwanted in New York."

"The place can be savage, that's true." Despite endless ribbing from his colleagues and friends, Richard had sold his Manhattan flat ten years prior and had moved to a sprawling house on Long Island. He still whined about the commute for his conducting gigs and the lack of good eating outside of the city but claimed the fresh air (on *Long Island?*) did him good. Barbecue tools in hand, he remained planted in his three-bedroom Cape Cod. "Listen, darling, we've all been sapped by a bad day in the city. But Sadie, dear, you *love* New York and New York loves you. Maybe she needs a reminder but I can't imagine the best thing to do is to up and leave. To godforsaken Iowa, no less."

"Perhaps you're right." I pulled off my knee-high brown suede boots and winced. Ever one to choose beauty over comfort, I remained willing to pay the price, physical and financial, for stunning footwear. "But if not teaching in Iowa, what, exactly is an out-of-work, past-prime opera singer to do?"

A click on the phone line interrupted Richard's response. "Sadie, honey," he said. His tone had changed to … giddy? "I need to take this call. Can I call you back?"

I rolled my eyes. "I thought you said you were single."

"Precisely why I need to take this call."

I heard the smile in his voice and had to laugh, happy for the thousandth time that I'd kept the toaster receipt. "Go. I'll call you in a few days."

"Don't make any decisions tonight," he said and clicked over to Bunny or Tiffani or Lola the showgirl.

I folded my phone shut and stretched out my tired limbs on the sofa. My eyes drifted closed and I didn't open them again until dawn.

3

Holy Night

I was what you might call an accidental Christian. My parents, East Coast transplants from a small town in North Dakota, were brought up with the fear of God, tornados, and Martin Luther. They passed these convictions on to their only child, a girl with more interest in performing one-act operettas in the church basement for the ruffians who stole the communion bread than singing in a secluded choir loft, behind the congregation and out of sight of potential admirers. To my parents' consternation, I disavowed church attendance from the day I left their home until Mother and Dad were both old and gray. My mother in particular seemed to find great comfort in my "coming around" when I started singing for pay in an imposing and well-attended Episcopal church in Manhattan just before she died. I think Mother thought I'd returned to the fold when, in fact, I was merely adding more shoe money to my monthly income.

The Church universal had its share of dirty laundry. Followers of Jesus toted around some cultural baggage—the Crusades, the Inquisition, the televangelists, and that was just for starters. Despite those prickly thorns—so awkward in ecumenical settings—Christmas Eve resurfaced each December as one time when I was happy to be Christian. For one thing, the music had no parallel. Even the most calloused of souls had to feel *something* when Handel proclaimed the child born and celebrated with a chorus of hallelujahs. "Silent Night," though sacrificed on the altar of popular music every year, remained the world's perfect lullaby. And "Joy to the World" offered endless possibilities for decorative soprano descants. Richard wrote several for me that I'd performed for everyone from the Unitarians ("let *all* [not just men] their songs employ") to a gig a few years ago with the Brooklyn Tabernacle Choir (add percussion, clapping, and an ocean of swaying).

At St. Mark's Episcopal on the Upper East Side, the Christmas mood was subdued. The sanctuary opened its arms to a legion of good-looking people in furs and precision haircuts. The smell of old money mingled sweetly with fresh-cut pine branches, trucked in from somewhere upstate. Decorative bunches woven with holly filled the space and brought to mind Bing, Nat, and Perry. For that evening's service, the organist and I had whipped up "O Holy Night" as a nod to a heavy tither who'd made her request known to the senior pastor. I'd warned Mavis, the organist, in no uncertain terms, that though I would perform the piece, neither she nor the philanthropist should expect any Celine Dion–inspired yelping. Mavis hadn't been able to hide her disappointment, but I stood my ground and we rehearsed the number accordingly.

I sat near the pulpit, resplendent in a cabernet-colored raw silk dress that hugged my figure in the bodice and then dropped into a lusciously full skirt. I had my father's height but was also grateful for my mother's contributions, most notably her shapely legs. Also gifted to me were Father's blue eyes, Mother's black hair. Father's impatience with imperfection, Mother's distrust of the government. Throw in my own original neuroses, and the result was one heck of a genetic cocktail.

My position facing the congregation allowed for optimum appraisal of those in attendance. I saw Lily MacIntosh, cohost of ABS's *America This Morning*. Having met Lily on several occasions, I could report her to be an unabashedly cold person after eleven in the morning. The mayor and his family arrived early, though I'd not yet seen Mr. and Mrs. Mayor interact. He stood at the narthex entrance, surrounded by a bevy of bodyguards, while she and their three pale and sullen children huddled together in a row near the front. Poor Mrs. Mayor. Even with the makeover team's intervention after her husband was sworn in, after the shellacked Jackie O. coiffure, crisp tweeds, and a softer shade of lipstick, the mayor's wife never seemed to look like she'd signed up for the job. She sat with an arm around one of her urchins, her expression more appropriate for Maundy Thursday than Christmas Eve.

Mavis launched into a contemplative and dissonant prelude of "We Three Kings."

I felt a hand on my shoulder.

"Two minutes, Sadie." Reverend Stephens smiled down at me before moving to take a seat on the other side of the pulpit. I watched him adjust the microphone on his skin-colored headset and then fiddle with the small control box attached underneath his vestments. The Reverend was about my age, well-regarded by his flock, and a good storyteller. His sermons entertained enough to keep my attention but were harmless enough to keep from offending his notoriously prickly congregation.

Nevertheless, should I ever find the need for a pastor type in times of need, I knew I'd never call on him. A few years back, I'd run into Stephens coming out of a five-star with his wife, both of them dressed to the hilt and the Reverend making a point to show me the new Tiffany bracelet he'd just given Mrs. Stephens for an anniversary gift. Call me a traditionalist, and perhaps I was out of the loop as far as trends among those of the cloth, but I liked my clergy to look a bit more monastic. Fine if they lost the hood and rope belt—but Tiffany's?

Mavis's "We Three Kings" ended in an unresolved chord and she nodded at Stephens to begin.

He stood and strode to the pulpit in polished Prada wingtips. Opening his arms wide to his parishioners, he said, "Welcome, children of God, to this most holy night when we anticipate together the advent of Christ Jesus."

The mayor hustled down the central aisle, bodyguards filing behind, and scooted into the row by his wife. Mrs. Mayor and the urchins didn't even glance in his direction.

"… And so let us sing together hymn 124, 'It Came Upon a Midnight Clear.'"

Mavis swooped in with an introduction and Stephens invited the congregation to stand. My position on the marbled stage elevated me slightly but I remained well within earshot of a crooning woman in a ghastly velvet number with matching hat. She sang from her spot in the second row, staring straight at me as if to make all those hours with some poor penniless vocal teacher worth her while. To compensate for the Velveteen Rabbit's wild vibrato on the chorus, I resorted to lip-synching. Who, I ask you, needed dueling sopranos on the eve of Christ's birth?

A tone-deaf baritone joined the crooner for "Angels We Have Heard On High," the two of them going for broke on the *glorias*. By the final verse, I was thinking of a safe place with padded walls, right when my upper register should have been soaring to the tops of the Gothic spires. Instead, I closed my eyes and tried to look serene as I listened to the final chorus before Stephens's short sermon.

"Why a baby?" he asked when the congregation had been seated. "A dependent, vulnerable babe, the Son of the Most High God. A dirty manger in an overcrowded town, two teenaged and scandalized parents, and the Son of the Most High God. The smell of animals, a group of ragtag, blue-collar shepherds, and the Son of the Most High God."

The mayor cleared his throat, bothered perhaps by recent union strikes and his office's blunders in the negotiations. A group of ragtag, blue-collar workers *can* cause quite a ruckus.

"In our culture, we are not taught the value of humility," Stephens continued. "Be more, do more, make more, we say to ourselves. Entertain us, appease us, and serve us, we say to our politicians."

There, that gave the mayor a boost. He sat up in his pew. Mrs. Mayor slumped.

"Work faster, work longer, work harder, we say to our children, because we can't let the world pass us by. We need to be noticed. We need to be affirmed. We look to the world to tell us our value and are fearful of the day when no one is watching anymore."

I bit the inside of my lower lip. Did someone tell Stephens about my sales numbers?

"And in the midst of this madness, we are visited by the Son of the Most High God, who turns the world on its end. Not more for abundance's sake, He says, but more to give to those in need. Not fame for fame's sake, but fame to spread God's love. This baby of whom the angels sing teaches us not to seek our own way and covet the praise of others but rather to seek humility, starting at the foot of a humble manger."

I shifted in my seat. This was a bit much. Wasn't Christmas about pretty presents and peace and goodwill? Friends, family, and mistletoe? Where was all the good cheer? Since when did Bling Man think we were here to get our consciences pummeled? I glimpsed Lily MacIntosh trying to be discreet with her Blackberry and I wished I were, for once, nestled in a pew with the others instead of up on display.

Stephens launched into a treatise on social activism and I began to relax. If nothing else, I was a friend of the charity ball circuit. My thoughts had wandered to a favorite and insanely overpriced boutique in SoHo when my eyes drifted to movement in the back of the sanctuary. A man who looked like he was there to audition for the part of John the Baptist or Tom Hanks in *Castaway* entered and stood while a disgruntled row in back inched over to make room. It was Christmas, after all, so one could hardly make him sit on the floor. But judging by the sour expression of a little girl sitting near him, I gathered the man's aroma overpowered that of the pine branches. He leaned over and rested his hands on his knees, eyes fixed on Stephens and brow furrowed in concentration.

The sermon concluded and after a brief prayer, I stood and stepped forward as Mavis began the rolling chords of the introduction. One phrase in and I knew I was in remarkably good voice that evening, even for me. People smiled as I sang, a young couple near the front huddled closer to each other and joined hands. Lily even stopped with the Blackberry.

I finished the first verse and my eyes drifted again to the back of the room. John the Baptist had risen from his seat. But instead of turning to go, as I'd assumed, he walked slowly down the center aisle. His eyes did not waver from mine, even with the rustle and twitter of people on both sides of the aisle as he made his way toward me. My hands became clammy and I began to worry he would just keep on walking right up to the stage, those intense eyes staring at me right before he ate me for breakfast. One of the mayor's bodyguards stood from his pew and seemed to be weighing the pros and cons of taking out a man whose only crime at this point was ruffling the feathers of convention. I cleared my throat and stood straighter. This man was not going to be the source of my first and only fold during a performance.

"Fall on your knees," I sang with authority.

The man smiled, looking as if those were exactly the words he'd been waiting for. And right there, in a room full of New York City high rollers, he lowered himself slowly, down to his knees, and bowed his head. The dark, drab gray of his clothing collapsed into a muddy pool of submission, stark in contrast to the colorful and wealthy sea that surrounded him on either side. He lifted his open hands in a small gesture, bringing them to rest in front of him as if he were letting water run through his fingers.

I caught my breath in the middle of a phrase.

Fall on your knees.

I stopped singing.

Fall on your knees.

The words rang in my ears, disorienting me until the velvet woman in front cleared her throat loudly. I gathered myself to finish the piece, though only through sheer force of will could I sing any words other than the ones that had brought that man to put his knees to the ground. The song was a command, though I'd never heard it that way. And I had certainly not thought it applied to me. Shepherds, yes. But not me. In a room full of people who were faithful to max out their 401(k)'s, monitor the nanny's hours, and keep up their appearances in the Hamptons, this man fell on his knees without a care of what they thought of him.

I finished the piece and stood still at the front of the room. Stephens touched my elbow and I remembered to return to my chair. When I sat down and looked up the center aisle, the man was gone.

It was not my practice to go looking for signs and wonders. After all, one could find just about anything if one looked hard enough. That Christmas Eve, I had not come to church looking, certainly not for a sign to leave the home I loved to travel to what I thought would be the ends of the earth, no stable in sight.

But for days afterward, the words and images pestered me. The unusually provocative sermon on humility, the man falling to his knees before a newborn baby king, the disconcerting feeling that a homeless man in Velcro sneakers had a better idea of the whole picture than I did.

Within four days, I'd called Avi and booked a flight for the unknown.

4

Tall Corn State

"Folks, we're about ten minutes from touchdown. Weather in Maplewood is nippy this afternoon. We're looking at seventeen degrees with winds out of the northwest at twenty miles an hour. Buckle up and get ready to button up!"

Was it a requirement in pilot training to talk like a game show host? I tossed back the remaining drops of my drink. I clutched the shreds of a Heartland Air cocktail napkin in both hands and focused my mind on unloading all my building angst onto our saccharine pilot and his solitary flight attendant, Beverly. Perhaps in an effort to counterbalance her cohort in the cockpit, Beverly was aviation's version of a truck stop waitress.

"You done?" she said, nodding to my empty wine glass. Beverly appeared to have plucked all of the eyebrows God gave her only to draw them back in with an orange eyebrow pencil.

I smiled. "Yes, thank you." I handed her my glass. "Tell me, Beverly. Are you based in Maplewood?"

Beverly's pretend brows shot into an impressive crop of bangs. "I most certainly am not. I live in Chicago. Have since I was a kid and don't plan on moving any time soon." She swiveled a half turn to collect an empty ginger ale can from the traveler across the row. Before moving on, she dropped her head and shoulders nearly into my lap and said in a stage whisper, "And if I were to move, you can bet your bippy it wouldn't be to *Iowa*." She snorted.

The woman across the aisle from me cleared her throat and shot a look at Beverly's retreating rump.

To be fair, by that point in the flight I had tried Beverly's patience just a wee bit. It was an exhaust issue. We were flying on a plane that should have been retired sometime after the Great War. I'd been forced into this, as Heartland Air was the only carrier flying into Maplewood. The. Only. One. I'd flown JFK to Chicago and then been routed to an obscure part of O'Hare known only to select airport employees and Iowans. The flight was to last less than an hour, but I spent the first thirty minutes having to use my portable air purifier to free my lungs of the stench.

"Whatcha got there, ma'am?" Beverly had asked when she saw me pull it out of my carry-on.

"Air purifier," I gasped, pushing the knob up to the highest setting. The fumes were overtaking the cabin and

I could *not* understand how the other passengers could sit idly by, content to page through the latest issue of *SkyShop* in search of a new inflatable mattress.

Beverly narrowed her eyes, a band of green eye shadow clearly visible on each lid. "They let that thing through security?"

I nodded and closed my eyes. *Think purity. Think O_2. Do not asphyxiate on a plane headed for Middle-earth.*

Beverly shook her head slowly. "I'm pretty sure the FAA would prohibit something like that. One false move and, were you so inclined, you could turn that puppy into a weapon."

I let out a long exhale. *I lived through September 11 while Bev was watching clips on the Today show, and she wanted to lecture me about security risks?* "I assure you, I took my *air purifier* through all the x-rays. I was even frisked in Chicago. I'm safe." I took another drag of pure air.

Beverly straightened and put her hand on her hip. "Well. I suppose as long as you keep it to yourself." She made two fingers into a V and pointed to her eyeballs. "But I'm keeping my eye on you."

The stench lifted halfway through the flight, though Beverly remained vigilant each time she passed my seat. Six years into the era of homeland security and Eagle Eye Bev was one of our more visible successes.

The plane banked to the left, giving me my first aerial view of Maplewood. Not an encouraging sight. The town held a little potential to be charming in a desperate, Mitford sort of way. I could make out a church spire and a bell tower, which appeared to be part of Moravia's campus. Clusters of residential areas circled the campus.

From my vantage point, I saw a total of six traffic lights. Be assured that I counted.

The outskirts of town held even less promise. Enormous machines, probably having to do with harvesting flax or something in that vein, spotted wide-open lots. Shades of gray dominated the color palette, with no break in the scheme for miles upon miles. No, wait: as the plane dropped in altitude I could make out small piles of hardened snow, which, though technically gray, I, in my magnanimity, chalked up as white. Gray and white and Sadie Maddox. One of these things was sure to kill the others.

I resisted the urge to cling to Beverly when the plane landed. We disembarked single file.

"Have a good one," Beverly said. She stood in the service area near the cockpit, arms crossed over an ample, cardigan-ed bosom.

"Thank you," I said, my voice sounding much like a boy soprano's. I tried again, volume and false confidence up a notch. "You have a good day too, Beverly."

She sniffed. "I will as soon as we're back up in the air and headed home."

Home, I thought. As I climbed through the chilly gate and walked toward baggage claim, home felt very far away.

♪

The fifteen or so passengers from Heartland Air Flight 2301 stood milling around the single baggage carrel.

Maplewood Regional Airport was more of a glorified garage. On my way to baggage claim, I'd passed one other gate, a set of restrooms, and a small nook where one could choose from a startling selection of beef jerky. No one had stepped forward from the small crowd of people waiting to welcome passengers so I stood alone looking for my bags. The air in the airport/garage was rather chilly and I was glad I'd worn my mink.

I fished my phone out of a new Gucci, a departure gift to myself, and waited for Richard to answer.

"Sadie?"

"Hello, Richard. I just wanted you to know I made it okay." I lowered myself into a chair.

"And how's Green Acres looking these days?"

"Sparse. Gray." I glanced at the faces in the luggage crowd and lowered my voice. "They're staring at me."

"Probably fascinated by the wild animal from New York. What are you wearing?"

"Choo boots, Saint Laurent black trousers, my mink, Dolce sunglasses."

Richard sounded like he was choking. "Good Lord, Sadie. You might as well be wearing a *hijab*."

I sighed. "Richard, what have I done?"

"So the John the Baptist incident at your church is finally losing some of its afterglow."

I'd cited the "O Holy Night" moment of clarity when I'd told Richard of my decision to take the job at Moravia. I had failed to mention the added incentive of a dwindling balance in my savings account. Avi had droned on mercilessly about my failure to plan for my retirement, my need to be stowing more away for the proverbial winter of the body. I admitted I'd been a horrible squirrel. Saving, in my opinion, had never been as much fun as *acquiring*. Nevertheless, when it came to choosing between curbing my spending and taking a semester's leave to the cornfields, I'm afraid I just didn't have the strength for that kind of self-denial. And so the reluctant relocation.

I felt the sting of tears and kept my sunglasses right where they were. "Thank you, Richard, for your encouragement. You've always known just the right thing to say."

Richard cleared his throat, which I knew was his attempt to take me seriously. "Sadie, love, listen. You're having an adventure, that's what. You're going to see an area of the country that is, though completely neglected by civilized people, a point of much anthropological interest. Think of it as a humanitarian effort. Think Mother Teresa."

"So I've landed in Calcutta."

"No, no, of course not." Richard paused. "That would mean you could get good ethnic food." He cackled at his own joke.

I closed my eyes behind my sunglasses. "You are not helping."

"You'll be fine," Richard said, trying very hard to sound persuasive. "You'll mold young minds, educe great music out of what appears to be a lost cause, and be back in New York with a renewed sense of purpose and a packed recital schedule in no time. I have a call in to Judith—"

"Ms. Maddox?"

I opened my eyes and saw before me a small white woman with an afro. She wore enormous Smurf-blue frames *à la* Sally Jessy Raphael, circa 1989. I signed off with Richard and stood to my feet. "Yes, I'm Sadie Maddox."

The woman smiled broadly and pushed her glasses up her nose. "Wonderful, wonderful. I'm so sorry to be late. My name is Miranda Ellsworth. I'm the music department secretary at Moravia College." She thrust out her hand.

I took it and she shook vigorously. The woman was in desperate need of moisturizer. "A pleasure to meet you, Ms. Ellsworth," I said. The baggage carrel lurched into motion and pieces of luggage began lumbering around the conveyor belt. "Ah, good. Excuse me while I get my luggage." I made a move toward the bags but was stopped by Ms. Ellsworth.

"Oh, no, we couldn't possibly—Cal will help with that, won't you, dear? You just point, Ms. Maddox."

A man who must have been standing nearby the whole time emerged to offer his hand.

"Cal Hartley," he said, voice gruff and eyes meeting mine. He looked to be in his mid-thirties, tight crop of chestnut hair, cheeks ruddy from the cold. He gripped my hand, shook once and walked to the baggage carrel. In one fell swoop, he lifted my two Louis Vuitton suitcases off the moving belt and was back by Ms. Ellsworth's side. He looked at my bags and raised his eyebrows at me as if to say, *did I choose correctly?*

I nodded. *All right, all right,* I thought. *So my luggage stands out too.*

"Truck's out front." Cal gestured for Ms. Ellsworth to lead the way. I followed like an obedient schnauzer.

"Did you have a nice flight, then?" Ms. Ellsworth

took my elbow when we got outside. I was at least twenty years her junior but perhaps she thought we city folk weren't used to icy sidewalks.

"I did, thank you." An image of Beverly and her "eyebrows" skittered across my mind and I wished I'd made friends with her. Perhaps she would have offered me a place to stay in Chicago and I could commute to Iowa. We picked our way across an icy mound on our passage across the street. Cal had parked his black pickup in what most airports would have reserved for a high-grossing ticket zone. Cal's truck, the only vehicle there, had been left running and unlocked.

Cal heaved my luggage into the back of the pickup bed and came to open the passenger door.

"I'll sit in back," Ms. Ellsworth said, gathering her polyester pants up a notch before scrambling into the back seat in one swift, afro-ed motion. I stood staring at the good three feet I'd need to mount before getting my body up into the seat. Curse it that I'd quit yoga.

"Need some help?" Cal asked, and I thought I saw the slightest hint of a smile forming around his eyes. He offered me his hand. I took it and he helped steady me as I pulled myself up into the cab of the truck. My rear hung off the edge of the seat for a few graceless moments. I hoped Cal was distracted by the mink. "Thank you," I said, smoothing my hair as he slammed the door shut. Lovely first impression I was making.

The frame of the truck lowered a bit; I could see Cal in the bed securing my luggage for the ride.

"Ms. Maddox, we are *thrilled* to have you join us for the semester," Ms. Ellsworth said. She'd edged her upper body into the space between the driver's and passenger's seats. "You have a lot of fans at Moravia, let me tell you."

"Thank you, Ms. Ellsworth. I hope to be of some help." I could just hear Richard snorting at my attempt at humility.

Ms. Ellsworth cleared her throat. "There has been one small change of plans." She pushed her glasses further up the bridge of her nose. Perhaps a pair that weighed less than a kilogram would help with the slippage problem. "It's regarding your housing situation."

The dean of the college had worked out the details with Avi, but I'd been told I'd stay in a cozy two-bedroom bungalow within walking distance of campus. This had, in fact, been a point of solace to me during my last days in New York. I'd pictured myself curling up by a fire, retiring to a spacious and quiet home after a day's work, reading through the collected works of Jane Austen in my spare time.

"Is there a problem?" I asked, though the pit in my stomach was already clueing me in to her answer.

Ms. Ellsworth pursed her lips. "Well, yes, I'm afraid. The house we had in mind for you has been sold."

"Sold?"

Cal opened the driver's side door and swung himself up to the seat. He shifted into drive, not looking at either of us nor speaking a word.

"I'm so sorry," Ms. Ellsworth said. "It was some sort of an administrative mix-up. But don't worry." She reached out to pat my arm. Her translucent skin showed every purple vein. "Our Plan B is even better."

"Where will I be living?"

Ms. Ellsworth switched from patting me to patting

Cal on his shoulder. "With Cal and his family on their beautiful farm."

"A farm?"

Cal gave me a sideways glance. "Yes, ma'am. A pig farm."

I gripped the handle on my door. "I—" I said, and stopped to clear my throat. "I'm afraid that won't work. I've never lived on a farm."

"You're kidding." Cal's eyes sparkled with laughter, though his mouth stayed in the straightest of lines.

Ms. Ellsworth shifted in her seat, moving even farther into my personal space. "Cal's wife, Jayne, is a lovely girl. You'll get along splendidly, I just know it. She saw me in the grocery store last week when I was all a-flurry trying to find alternative arrangements for you. Jayne was such a doll and offered their attic, which I know you'll just love. It has lots of space and beautiful light. Jayne and Cal have fixed up that house so nice, haven't you, Cal?"

Cal nodded slowly. He seemed like a man who needed very little conversation, certainly not with Sally Jessy or a woman who required help getting into his truck.

I turned to face Ms. Ellsworth. "I don't mean to be rude, but is there a hotel in town? I'd hate to impose in someone's home."

"Oh, it's no imposition at all," Ms. Ellsworth said, dismissing the thought with the wave of a veiny hand. "And as for a hotel, I'm sure there will be openings sometime after spring break. I'm afraid we have only one hotel in town and it's booked solid with conference folks and parent visits until then."

Last time I consulted a college calendar, spring break

didn't hit until at least March, two months away. I looked out the window and wondered how much damage I'd incur on my mink were I to open my door and roll away from the truck as it sped toward its home on a pig farm.

I watched small gray hills blend into more small gray hills and wished for a paper bag in which to inhale. *Bad karma*, I thought mournfully. I closed my eyes, reliving all the times I was late to rehearsals, snippy about a conductor, demanding with contract negotiations. *And my blasted fortieth birthday*, I moaned inwardly. I *knew* I should have acknowledged it, thrown a red hat or purple boa party or whatever. Some celestial being was punishing me for pretending it didn't even happen. *Fine, I get it! I'll be nice from now on—I promise!*

"Ms. Maddox, are you all right?" Ms. Ellsworth popped her head around my shoulder. "You just, *ehm*, moaned."

I'd forged little purple teeth marks into a knuckle on my right hand. "Did I?" I let my hand rest on the seat beside me. Ms. Ellsworth went back to her patting, this time my shoulder.

Soon we turned off the highway and onto a gravel road. Ahead of us loomed a large white farmhouse with red shutters and window boxes. In any other circumstances, a photo in *National Geographic*, say, the house would have struck me as curious, Norman Rockwellian even. But an odor was filtering through the car vents that accosted my every sense.

I was trapped, trapped in a land impervious to air purifiers.

Cal cut the engine and looked over at me. "Welcome to the country."

5

Habitat

I was glad for Cal's help out of that blasted truck because by the time he'd cut the engine at the end of the gravel driveway, I was feeling lightheaded. Ms. Ellsworth was chittering about the wallpaper job she'd undertaken in her own home, and I couldn't possibly feign interest so I kept my mouth shut. Cal opened my door and helped me down before turning to give a hand to Ms. Ellsworth.

"... A pretty yellow floral print, see, which was just *perfect* with the slip covers but Ed said he couldn't get the three rolls I needed to his store for at least another six weeks and I ..."

And so on and so forth while we picked our way over frozen mud toward a set of stairs on the side of the house.

I had a death grip on Cal's arm and kept my nose buried in my coat to ward off the frigid temperatures and the stench that permeated the air around the house. I peeked out of my little cocoon and looked toward the barn, sure my eyes would be greeted with a slew of swine. Not a pig in sight. We shuffled onward, Ellsworth yipping and yapping along behind us.

Cal opened the door and a gush of warm air washed over us as we stepped into a bright kitchen. Children were scattered everywhere, all of them in some stage of running with the exception of a baby who was busy coating herself and her high chair with applesauce. A woman yelled in some other part of the house.

"Drew Jonas Hartley, you put that ax down right now. I do not want to have to tell your father you hit your brother over the head with it."

Oh, sweet Lord, I thought. *I'm in hell.*

"Babe?" Cal called. He politely uncurled my fingers from his sleeve and bent over to untie his boots. "Company's here." A swarm of children ran into the kitchen and jumped on Cal's back, shouting indecipherable greetings.

Jayne rounded the corner into the kitchen, yet another child squirming in her arms. She smiled and blushed furiously. "Cal," she said, "I thought you said you'd ring the doorbell." She walked toward me and put out her hand. "I'm Jayne Hartley. Welcome to our home."

"Thank you," I said, doing my best to smile. "I'm still quite surprised to be here."

"Pow! Pow-pow-pow *pow!*" A boy as tall as the countertops careened around the kitchen shooting his fingers. "You're dead!" he said to Cal.

"Not funny, young man," Cal said and the boy stopped in his tracks. "Put the guns away."

"Yes, sir," the boy said and ran with another boy out of the room. I heard a thud and one of the boys started wailing. Cal left to investigate.

Ms. Ellsworth was in the corner with the high chair baby talking in a high-pitched voice. She turned to my hostess. "Jayne, Ms. Maddox was concerned this would be an imposition."

"Oh, goodness, no," Jayne said. Her eyes were the color of cornflower and framed with dark eyelashes. She pushed a strand of her pale blonde bob behind her ear. "You're no trouble. We enjoy company."

How on earth that was true with an entire elementary school already living under one roof, I certainly didn't know.

"Ms. Maddox," Ms. Ellsworth said. She was shoveling a spoonful of what appeared to be gruel into the baby's mouth. My stomach turned. "She might not have the courage to tell you herself so I will." She nodded toward Jayne. "Our Jaynie has a lovely singing voice herself. Had a solo in the Maplewood High Swing Choir all four years."

Jayne let the squirming child out of her arms. He ran out of the kitchen as soon as his feet hit the linoleum. "Miranda, please." Jayne shook her head and looked down at her hands. "That was a long, long time ago." She looked up and gave me a small smile. "Ms. Maddox, I so enjoy your work. You have"—she took a deep breath and her voice got small—"you have a wonderful instrument."

"Thank you, Jayne," I said, wondering how a pig

farmer's wife got a hold of Deutsche Grammophon recordings. "I'd love to hear you sing as well."

She looked horrified.

Cal came back into the kitchen holding a little boy in each arm.

Ellsworth kissed the applesauce child on the cheek. "Well, I'll let you folks get settled. Cal, you mind putting those boots back on and giving me a ride back to town?"

Cal nodded and looked at his wife. "I'll take the older two with me. We'll be back for dinner in an hour."

An hour? It took sixty minutes to get to town and back? Was he crossing Midtown during rush hour? I felt the lightheadedness return. A half-hour's drive from a ten-thousand-person metropolis, and I had *chosen* this.

Ms. Ellsworth embraced me. I hadn't realized how short she was until her nose was buried in my sternum. She pulled back, eyes suddenly bright with tears. "We are so honored to have you in Maplewood, Ms. Maddox." She bit her lower lip. "If I may speak for our department, I want you to know this is a dream come true."

I gulped, feeling just a tad guilty for wondering about return flights leaving in the morning. "I appreciate your kindness, Ms. Ellsworth."

She took a handkerchief from her pocket and blew her nose loudly enough to make it squeak. "Well," she said, turning to Cal and the boys. Jayne had suited them up in coats that made them immobile. Oversized stocking caps shrouded their eyes.

"Shall we?" Ellsworth said.

Jayne closed the door behind them and took my coat from a hook by the door. "I'll show you upstairs."

A half hour later, I stood at the top of the attic stairs and waited for Jayne to shut the door at the bottom. I hurried to the bed and began rummaging around in my purse for my cell. After punching in the number, I lowered myself onto an upholstered chair by one of two large windows. First ring. Jayne's footsteps receded until I could only hear the occasional high-pitched yell of a child. Second ring. If he didn't answer, I'd hurl myself off—

"Avi Feldman."

"Oh, thank God. Avi, it's me. Sadie."

"Sadie! Speak of the mezzo devil herself. I'm at dinner with Marc, Alyanna, and Michelle, and we were just talking about you."

I heard some giggling in the background. "Avi, there's been a mix-up with my accommodations. You have to help."

"What is it, love? Wait—let me move to a quieter spot. You know Lime at this hour on a Thursday."

Oh, did I ever. My mouth watered to think of one bite of their *picadillo*, washed down with a *mojito*. I would wither out here in the land of Velveeta.

"Okay. I can hear you. What's this about the bungalow?" Avi's voice was still inappropriately loud but I suspected most things would seem that way out here in God's country.

"They sold the bungalow."

"Who sold it?"

"I don't know. The college realtor. And there's no room in the lone hotel until late March."

"You can't be serious. I'll call them."

"Please, Avi."

"Where are you now?"

I sighed. "On a pig farm."

There was a slight pause and then laughter. "I'm sorry," Avi said, gathering himself. "It's just such an incongruous picture: famous soprano meets"—and he snorted here—"swine and slop." He broke into new peals of giggles.

"You laugh like a girl," I snapped. I'd begun to pace the length of the attic. "Is this why I pay you twenty percent?"

He sobered immediately. "There's no need to get personal, love. I'll call the college tomorrow and see about another rental house. And I'll ask about the hotel in the meantime. I'll take care of it, Sadie. Don't think about it again until we talk tomorrow."

"Easy for you to say. You aren't sleeping in the attic."

"Oh, you are *not*." He lowered his tone to dish. "Is it creepy? Do you think it's haunted?"

"Do you imagine yourself to be a helpful person?"

"Is it an old house?"

"At least a century."

Avi whistled. "Jews don't believe in exorcisms and such but I might recommend calling upon the nearest Catholic. Just to be safe."

I massaged the bridge of my nose with my fingers. "Avi, I don't know if I can do this." I squeezed my eyes shut but hot tears brimmed through my lashes.

"Oh, Sadie, of course you can." Avi was quiet a moment, and then, "Are you crying?"

"Of course not," I said. I wiped both cheeks with the back of my hand. Turn it on, turn it off—that was one grace earned after a life of performing. "I'm just tired." I cleared my throat and dabbed on a little confidence. "I'll talk with you tomorrow. Think results, agent-who-got-me-into-this-mess."

"Positive thinking, love. Keeps the spirits at bay."

I clicked the phone shut. A quilt cushioned my collapse on the bed where I could lie and let the tears fall as they would. *I should have just said no to Avi,* I thought. What did he know, anyway? So I had a few unpaid bills. So I hadn't nabbed the typical concert lineup. Everyone had off seasons. When had it become a good business decision to run with one's tail between her legs toward the nearest stretch of wilderness?

One hotel, I moaned to myself, awash in a fresh wave of tears. I was living in a town with one hotel. Cecilia Bartoli was likely, in that very moment, ordering room service in a Four Seasons and I was waiting in a drafty attic for a cowbell to announce the call for "supper."

Fully absorbed in my luxurious self-pitying, I propped myself up on a pillow to take stock of my surroundings. I blotted my eyes with a tissue and looked around the room.

Ms. Ellsworth had been right. Jayne and Cal did have a lovely home, if one were in the market for pig farmhouses. Jayne had led me through the dining room and living area, up one flight of stairs, past a cove of bedrooms, then up one more flight to the attic. Jayne had picked her way nimbly through all three floors, over toys, puzzles, games, and dolls. I'd nearly broken my neck on a disjointed train track while listening to Jayne's

tour. She'd said the house had been in Cal's family since
his great-grandfather had built it. Its polished oak floors,
wraparound porch, and yawning picture windows had
me wondering if a wayward Walton would come around
the corner calling for John-Boy.

We'd accessed the set of stairs leading to the attic
through a small door. I barely missed the threshold
without grazing the top of my head. Jayne had taken the
steps two at a time, the baby giggling on her hip. She
wasn't even breathing hard, whereas I was hoping for an
oxygen tank waiting at the summit. What with the truck
vaulting and the stair climbing, I'd be in decathalon
condition after a semester in the Midwest.

Jayne had gestured to the room. "Well, here we are,"
she said shyly. "It's all ready for you."

I sat back on the bed now and rubbed the bottom
of my left foot with both hands. The space from one
end of the attic to the other was larger than my first two
apartments. Cal and Jayne had painted the walls of their
home in a warm and fresh palette of colors, a welcome
relief after hearing Ms. Ellsworth go on about her floral
wallpaper. My tour through the rest of the house had
glimpsed apple green, tangerine, aquamarine, and
chocolate brown. This room was the crown and painted
terracotta with eggshell trim. I looked out the window
nearest the bed and figured my view encompassed most
of Iowa and half of whatever state it butted up against.

I took a shaky breath and a break from rubbing
my toes to stand and stretch. At the end of the room, a
door opened to a small restroom, an afterthought, Jayne
said, when Cal had figured out the plumbing would
be possible. I was grateful for the decision to include a

private commode, as the idea of sharing a toilet with all those little bladders sent shivers down my spine.

I checked my watch and saw I should begin the descent to the dinner table. Jayne had insisted I rest and not try to help preparing the meal. My weak protest went unheeded, a fortuitous circumstance for the Hartleys, as they escaped my cooking. Richard had once accused me of trying to poison him. I rose from the bed and took one more look out the window. A tepid winter sun was setting over a barren field. I'd never in my life seen so much open space, each millimeter of it touched by pale pink light. I wondered if people around here saw this as beauty or if, like me, the endless space made them feel wobbly, as if stranded on a tightrope when the wind was picking up. I turned to go downstairs and passed my bags, sitting at attention by the door, untouched and ready for a trip home, just in case.

6

Among the Natives

When we sat down to eat, I received my first good news of the day. Despite earlier worries to the contrary, the Hartleys had only three children. Their eldest was the ax wielder, Andrew. The gun shooter had been a school classmate who'd since been returned to town and to his own unfortunate family. That left the squirmer who couldn't seem to decide whether he wanted to be on Jayne's hip or not. This one was named Joel. The baby was parked once again in the high chair, the only girl and named Emmy.

"Her real name is Emmalie Rose Hartley," Andrew said. "But we call her Emmy for short. Short names are nicknames. My nickname is Drew. Joel's nickname is Joey. Daddy's nickname is Cal but his real name is Calvin. My mommy's nickname is Jaynie. What's your nickname, Miss Sadie?"

I was watching him and marveling. The child had mastered circular breathing.

"Drew, join hands with your brother and sister. Let's pray over our meal." Cal's deep baritone made even famous singers submit. I took Jayne's hand and bowed my head.

"Daddy, she's not holding Emmy's hand," Drew said in a stage whisper.

I looked up.

"That's all right," Cal said. "She's still getting used to us."

"Not at all," I said, clearing my throat. I put out my hand and hoped babies weren't capable of scratching off very expensive fingernail polish. She looked at me and banged both hands down on her tray. I jumped.

Jayne tried to hide her smile. "Cal, go ahead."

"Heavenly Father, we thank You for this day. Thank You for the winter that allows the land and those who take care of it to rest. Thank You, dear God, for starting everything over again from scratch. I suppose we all could use a fresh beginning now and then. We are grateful to You for noticing."

My heart started pounding like it did witnessing crazy hairy man on Christmas Eve. I told it to stop it already, worried about what could happen should I start making important life decisions every time crazy hairy man came to mind. Soon I'd be wearing a loincloth in the Amazon and teaching the natives how to read treble clef.

"Now please bless the food we're about to eat and bless the hands that prepared it. In Jesus' name, Amen."

"Amen!" the kids shouted, and mealtime commenced.

I'd grown up an only child so this kind of culinary experience was not unlike watching a PBS special. Jayne was so occupied with the feeding frenzy, I don't believe she ate a bite. I certainly didn't see it. Her children were just so *needy*.

"Mommy, milk," Joel said, holding his plastic cup up and letting it down with a bang.

"Mommy, milk, please," Jayne parroted, reaching for the cup.

"Pweeeeeeese," Joel said, then took the cup and spilled all of its contents.

"So, Ms. Maddox, tell us about what you all like to eat up in New York City." Cal was reaching across his plate to cut Drew's slice of ham, likely butchered on the back porch before he came to retrieve me from the airport.

I patted my mouth with a paper napkin. "Well," I said, shrugging, "New York was and continues to be built by people from all over the world. You can buy any kind of food imaginable, and often at all hours of the day."

Jayne reappeared from below the table where she'd been mopping up milk that had dripped between the cracks. She blew her bangs off her forehead and turned to me, eyes shining. "Like what? What's your favorite?"

I took a gulp of cold milk and wondered if these people milked their own cows, too. Much more disturbing, I wondered if touching udders would be required of guests. "For example, the block on which I live has restaurants serving food from Morocco, Ethiopia, northern Italy, Greece, and India. And that's just one block among hundreds."

Cal looked at me across the table, chewing thoughtfully. "What about normal food?"

I swallowed a mouthful of cheddar-bombed potatoes. "Well," I said, "to many people that food *is* normal, Cal."

The house hummed in Cal's silence. A furnace clunked around in the basement as it roared to life. Cal nodded slowly. "Not to me," he said, slicing off a wedge of ham that would have been the weekly protein allowance for a fashion model. "I want to know where I'd go if I wanted meat and potatoes. Normal food."

I glanced at Jayne. She was mired so deeply in the care of her children, Cal and I could have been discussing the strengths and weaknesses of the UN in the former Yugoslavia for all the opportunity she had to participate. I watched her butter three slices of bread rapid-fire and cut one into halves, one into fourths, and one into bite-sized chunks, all within the time in took Cal to finish his mouthful of ham.

I returned my gaze to the man of the house. "If you came to New York, Cal," I said, "I'd send you straight to Times Square for a neon-lit, bright lights, big city meal at ESPN Zone. Perfect for your appetite, I would imagine."

"Excellent," he said through a smile. He took a swig of milk. "Now you're speaking my language."

"Mommy, I'm finished." Drew slumped in his chair. "My tummy is *sooooo* full."

"Too full for dessert?" Jayne asked. She was feeding the baby spoonfuls of yogurt.

"No, I think I can fit some dessert," Drew said slowly, weighing the gravity of the task before him.

"If that's the case, you'll need to finish your dinner." Jayne pointed at the boy's half-empty plate with her spoon. "Five more bites of ham and three more of your potatoes. And finish the broccoli."

"Mommy," Drew whined. "I'm only hungry for dessert."

"You heard your mother," Cal said. "Dessert is only for people who eat the good stuff first."

Words to the wise, those were, because by following Cal's advice, the rest of us were granted a piece of Jayne's apple streusel pie.

"Jayne," I said, only one bite in and already breathless, "this is magnificent."

She blushed. "Thank you, Miss Sadie."

"Please, call me Sadie," I said, filling my fork with pastry.

"Okay," Drew said. "Sadie, would you pass the milk?"

"Not you, sir," Jayne said. "Sometimes grown-ups call each other by their first names but you stick with 'Miss Sadie.'"

"All done," Joel said from his position on the bench he shared with Drew. "'Ssert!"

"Please," Jayne said. Her dinner plate remained untouched.

"Pweese," Joel said, his eyes trained on her as she dished up a small slice of pie. Drew slumped in his chair and munched on a tree of broccoli.

"I'm serious, Jayne," I said. I had my nose down near the plate and was tempted to lick the remaining crumbs. "This crust would be worthy of a five-star restaurant in New York."

"Oh, you're just hungry for some home cooking," she said, cheeks red and eyes glistening.

Cal put down his fork. "Jayne comes home with blue ribbons from the state fair every year." He pushed back his chair. "Wait 'til spring and her rhubarb crisp." He leaned down to smooch her loudly on the cheek. The kids giggled.

"I'm not a very good cook," Jayne said, sawing into her now-cold ham. "But I've always loved to bake. My mother taught me how to make a piecrust when I was little and it just kind of grew from there."

I couldn't argue with her about the cooking, at least based on this evening's ho-hum performance. But I could swallow a great many bland calories on my way to a pie like that.

Drew reluctantly finished his "good stuff" and was given his reward. We passed some quiet minutes together, each of us reveling in the joy of a successfully flaky crust.

"May we be excused?" Drew spoke for both boys, who had become very efficient eaters when faced with their dessert.

"You may," Cal said.

"Bring your plates to the sink, please," Jayne called as they ran out of the room. They made a wide arc in the dining room and returned to the table.

"Your children obey you," I said, watching their plates wobble precariously until Cal intercepted them near the sink.

Jayne laughed. "We'll see what you have to say about that after a few weeks here." She stood to lift the baby out of her chair. "They've had lots of time-outs to get to this point."

"And bare-butt spankings," Cal said as he followed the boys into the family room.

Corporal punishment. Fantastic. I looked around for some more pie to comfort me.

Jayne rounded the table, jostling the baby on her hip. She reached to clear my plate and I thanked her. "I need to put Emmy to bed, but would you like some coffee or tea? I can put it on now before I go up."

"Tea would be lovely, thank you. But I can make it myself. Just point me to your teapot."

Jayne showed me the pot and then turned to go. When she got to the threshold, she turned and smiled. "Thank you for your compliments about the dessert, Sadie. It means a lot coming from you."

"It was the perfect end to a trying day," I said. I watched her go and wondered how long the glow from a piece of pie could be expected to last.

7

Maplewood

The amplified noise of my own breathing awakened me. I tugged gingerly on my velvet eye cover and squinted into pitch-blackness. During the night, primal instincts must have prompted me to flee the cold and burrow further and further under the quilts until I woke, my body pulled into a ball at the foot of the bed. I crawled back toward my pillow and braved one arm out of the cocoon in order to feel around on the bedside table for the alarm clock. My hand knocked off a tumbler of water. I cursed and pulled my entire upper body out of the covers. My lungs hurt, the air was so cold. The room was still dark, but the clock read seven-thirty. I groaned and pulled the covers back over my head. I must have fallen asleep because the next thing I remembered was a knock on the door at the foot of the stairs.

"Sadie?" Jayne said timidly when she'd opened the door a crack.

"*Hmmm?*" I said, forcing my eyelids open.

"I'm going into town pretty soon if you'd like to catch a ride to campus. Didn't you say you wanted to stop by the music building sometime today?"

"Yes," I whispered and then cleared my throat to say it more loudly. "I need an hour."

"An hour?" she asked. "Right. Okay. I'll just do some more laundry and get a meal in the Crock-Pot. Emmy will help." I could hear the baby babbling. "Emmy's coming, too, aren't you, sweetie?"

All right, I thought. *No baby talk before coffee.*

She shut the door and I willed my feet onto the cold floor. Frost lined the *inside* of the attic windows. I whimpered on my way to the bathroom and immediately turned on the shower to scalding. I stood in front of the mirror and waited for it to fog up before getting wet. The bags under my eyes had grown overnight. So much for fresh air being the victor in the fight against aging. I growled at my reflection, sneering at the idiot who had agreed to move out to the freezing little house on the forsaken prairie.

♪

Because some sense of mercy still remained in the world, Jayne did not drive a truck. She drove the equally alien but more physically accessible minivan. I shuffled down the walk as quickly as my Ferragamos would take me and slammed the door against the cold and the stench.

"Do you get used to that smell?" I asked Jayne through my scarf. I tried thinking of happy scents, like vanilla and cinnamon, but to no avail. Pigs put up a fight against even the wildest of imaginations.

"Smell?" Jayne clicked the final of seventeen buckles on Emmy's car seat. "Oh, the pigs. Yes, I suppose I am used to it." She positioned herself behind the wheel and we started up the driveway. "The summer is always a challenge. Heat's never a good thing for a manure pile."

My stomach turned at the thought. The scarf stayed right where it was, even though we were whizzing down the highway and away from the farm.

"It's too bad you're seeing Maplewood at this time of the year." Jayne nodded toward the pale expanse of fields that surrounded us. The wind howled against the car, blending in with Emmy's whimpers and making Jayne grip the steering wheel with white knuckles. "Spring is much prettier. You probably can't imagine it right now, but everything becomes green. Green so bright you have to squint."

She tossed a stuffed animal to the baby in back. Emmy looked a bit stunned but stopped crying and clutched the spotted dog that had been hurled to her rescue.

"You're right," I said, looking out my window. "It's very hard to imagine now." Sunlight would have helped. The sky was a transparent white, almost an absence of color. No clouds, no difference in texture or hue from one side of the horizon to another. "Did you grow up here, Jayne?"

"Yep," she said, signaling to turn right onto another endless stretch of highway. We'd been in the car ten minutes and still no sign of a convenience store, much less a college. "Cal and I started dating in high school. He's two years older, so he left first for State and I followed him when I graduated. We got married when he finished and moved back home two years later."

We crested a hill and saw the town of Maplewood below us. On the left a large limestone sign proclaimed Maplewood to be the home of Sauerkraut Days, Moravia College, and the Girls' State Basketball Champs of 1987. Jayne slowed as we entered town, turning north as soon as we reached the stop sign by Bud's Feed. I felt a sinking in my chest and thought of the sad migration of those pathetic people in *The Grapes of Wrath*. If Steinbeck had been alive, I would have called him to commiserate.

"How many people live in Maplewood?" I asked, barely resisting the urge to let my forehead fall on the window glass.

"Just a sec. Would you mind giving this to Emmy?" Jayne handed me a graham cracker. I turned in my seat and held it out for the baby. Emmy snatched it from my hand and made a sound that, in New York, would have meant she was getting mugged.

Jayne returned to my question. "Ten thousand or so. I think they say twelve thousand, counting the students and surrounding areas." She waved to a woman passing us on the sidewalk. "That's Anne Marie Morris. She owns the flower shop down the way."

I thought of the buckets of fresh flowers perpetually

stocked and ready for the taking in my corner grocery in New York. A pang of homesickness flooded over me. I looked out my window, knowing my face would betray my misery. After all, it wasn't Jayne's fault she knew nothing better. Born a Maplewoodian, destined to die one as well.

The center of town, labeled *Downtown Historic District* by helpful signs, offered a smidgen of promise. No need for subway plans, but at least I could see signs of life. We passed a hardware shop, a barbershop, and the town library. Students lined the steamed-up window seats at Wired, a coffee shop representing a sliver of hope. At least it wasn't Denny's. Most storefronts displayed Moravia's mascot, which looked to be a close cousin to the meerkat. The blocks right off the town square marred the view. Strips of seedier looking businesses—a grouchy looking gas station, an auto repair shop, a Subway badly in need of paint—hovered just outside the perimeter like a group of social misfits at the senior prom.

Perhaps it was the cold, but the people of Maplewood appeared to move in slow motion. Jayne would have been killed by now should she have driven like that down the streets of Manhattan. I glanced at the speedometer: We were racing through the historic district toward Moravia's campus, hovering the whole way just above six miles per hour. I didn't know the official speed limit, but none of the cars in the other lane seemed to be going any faster than my chauffeur.

"That was city hall. And there's the courthouse. Jill's Book Nook is on the corner, in case you're looking for some pleasure reading."

"Who's the man on the horse?" I pointed to a statue

on the edge of an abandoned park. A flock of swings danced a jagged waltz in the wind.

"Oh, that's Josiah Woods. Town founder and inventor of the safety pin."

Did I detect *pride* in her voice? "Very useful, the safety pin."

She nodded. "Isn't it, though? Believe it or not, I used to be so embarrassed about it. Other towns around here make fun. During ball games in high school, the other teams would call us the Maplewood Pinheads." She laughed. "Isn't that hilarious? I think it's funny now, but that was the beginning of a long phase of hometown-hating that I had to go through before coming back here."

We passed another stately limestone sign reading "Moravia College, Established 1894." The minivan crawled up a wide boulevard lined with trees, student housing peppering spacious lawns on either side. The windows of the dorms sported various levels of free speech, ranging from leftover strands of Christmas lights to a triumphant Bob Marley flag bedecked with marijuana leaves circling Marley's head. I stared at the buildings and the students returning from winter break, who lined the sidewalks and made it a sea of parkas, heads ducked into the wind and cold.

"It's been a long time since I was coed myself." I took a deep breath. "They'll probably eat me alive."

Jayne pulled to a stop in front of the Kjellman Fine Arts Building. She shifted into park and turned to me. "You'll be perfect." She smiled. I noticed light brown freckles that dusted her nose and cheeks. Jayne could have passed as a coed herself. "I'm sure of it."

I pulled on my gloves and braced myself for the walk to shelter inside a looming set of engraved doors. "Thanks for the ride. Ms. Ellsworth said she would take me back to your house when we're through."

I opened the door and took my first teetering steps back to academia.

8

Working Girl

Ms. Ellsworth greeted me in the administrative offices.

"Ms. Maddox," she said, hands extended in front of her as if she were Laura Bush welcoming me to the Oval Office. "Welcome to Moravia. I'm *so* excited this day has finally arrived." Instead of taking my hands, she clapped. "Here," she said, "let me take your coat."

I slid out of my honey-colored mid-length. She took it and *smelled it.*

"*Mmm.*" Her eyes rolled back into her head. "Forgive me, but I love the smell of fine clothes." She scanned the office, empty but for us, and lowered her voice. "You just let me know if you ever need to store your *fur.*" She winked and turned to her desk.

I closed my eyes and tried to think of a safe place.

"Well," she said briskly, hanging the coat carefully on the back of her chair, "let me show you to your office. It's a humble room, but I hope you like it. Your student assistant, Mallory, should have it ready for your arrival."

"Student assistant?" I asked.

Ms. Ellsworth locked the office door behind us and led the way down the corridor. "Mallory, yes. She's a dear. She'll help you get settled and will be your little helper for all administrative needs, photocopying, record keeping, and so forth. It's an open-ended assignment. You and she can decide the best way to use her time."

Well. My own assistant. Perhaps this was to be less provincial than I'd feared. I'd have to teach her how to make a decent cup of tea, but this was certainly a pleasant perk Avi had not mentioned.

Ms. Ellsworth beckoned me over to a closed set of double doors. "They're rehearsing—early rehearsal before classes resume—but I'm sure we can pop in."

Before I had a chance to say otherwise, she opened the door and a wash of a cappella choral music blanketed us. Ms. Ellsworth made a great show of tiptoeing over to a group of chairs sitting at the sidewall. I followed her, though at five-foot-ten, I've found it best not to tiptoe unless medically necessary.

The conductor's eyes were closed and he was lost in one particularly majestic passage of a Schumann piece. In a slow wave, the students allowed their eyes to flicker over to us, then nudged those next to them to continue the pattern. The conductor, a small, frightfully pale man with thinning white hair, eventually caught on to the distraction and gave a cutoff. He turned toward us with lively blue eyes and clasped his hands. Bounding off the podium in quick, energetic steps, he was at my side in seconds, offering his hand and bowing.

"Ms. Maddox," he said in a German accent, "it is my great honor." He kissed my hand and when he came back up, his eyes were glistening. "I am Gunther Reinhart, conductor of the Moravia College Concert Choir and your most loyal servant."

This was shaping up to be a lovely morning. "Thank you, Gunther. You know how to give an old opera singer a heroine's welcome."

"Old!" he yelped. He slapped one knee of his worn brown corduroys. "Ms. Maddox, I assure you, until you have reached my age of seventy-one, you may not speak the word." His eyes crinkled with mirth. "And even then, I forbid it."

Ms. Ellsworth cleared her throat. "Dr. Reinhart has built our choral department into an internationally recognized ensemble." She patted his hand. That woman and patting. "He's a treasure for us."

Dr. Reinhart smiled at Ms. Ellsworth. "Thank you, my dear. Did you know," he said, turning again to me, "that Miranda here was a second soprano in one of my first ensembles at Moravia?" He led me by the elbow to the center of the room.

"Singers," he said to the students, "this woman, as you know, needs no introduction from a wily foreigner like myself."

The students smiled. They seemed very familiar with the humor and speech of this endearing man who would certainly receive signed copies of my CDs within the week.

"But in case you have been sleeping and have not heard the news, it is my pleasure to introduce to you Moravia's newest faculty member, the exquisitely talented and equally beautiful Sadie Maddox."

Seriously, Avi was fired. I was taking the German back to New York.

The students clapped loudly, hooting and hollering and grinning like fools. I ate it up. So nice to be around a group of aspiring musicians, still fresh with passion and oblivious to the insurmountable odds most face in the business of making music. I smiled at them and put one hand on my heart, thanking them.

"Thank you," I said as the applause died down. "You are kind to give me such a warm welcome. I'm thrilled to be here and am greatly looking forward to working with many of you this semester." Out of the corner of my eye, I saw a pretty brunette alto in the first row shift on her feet and roll her eyes. When she saw me looking, her expression shifted to an ingratiating smile. I cleared my throat. "I'll leave you to your rehearsal. I know that an ensemble doesn't produce a sound like what I heard a few moments ago without a significant amount of practice."

Dr. Reinhart grabbed me by the shoulders and kissed me loudly on both cheeks. I stumbled back a step from the sheer force of his affection. He bowed again and said, "Thank you, Ms. Maddox. It is an honor to make music with you and for you."

The students twittered. I glanced at the shifty alto. She was whispering something into the ear of another girl.

Ms. Ellsworth came up behind me and led me by

the elbow out of the room. I could hear the Schumann resume as the doors closed behind us.

"He's quite the character," I said, taking a tissue from Ellsworth to wipe my cheeks.

She sighed. "We adore Dr. Reinhart. But I'm afraid he's become increasingly dramatic with the years. And much more physically affectionate." She turned to me, eyebrows raised. "He'll likely go for the lips next time."

I made a face. "Thanks for the warning."

She nodded. "Musical genius, but kind of like the crazy uncle in the departmental family. Just remember to turn your cheek."

Like Jesus, I thought, though I doubted He'd had crazy uncles in mind.

We passed a string of classrooms. I peered at the placards and the occupants readying themselves for the semester: a canary yellow music theory classroom haunted by a tall, impossibly thin man with big glasses; music history with a woman wearing a starched white blouse and orthopedic-looking shoes; percussion ensemble being taught by a woman in a purple muumuu and matching head scarf. Just past the classrooms, a tall Nordic-looking man approached us.

"Hello, Ms. Ellsworth," he said without looking in her direction. "Ms. Maddox, welcome. I am Kent Johannsen."

I took his hand. "A pleasure, Mr. Johannsen." For being a man of such stature, his handshake was weak and clammy. I let go.

"Kent teaches voice here as well," Ms. Ellsworth said. "And the occasional course of musical appreciation for the college at large."

Kent's penetrating stare was starting to give me the willies. I'd take Dr. Reinhart's questionable kissing any day.

"Well," he said, "I just wanted to introduce myself. I don't intend to keep you." A gush of inappropriate, breathy laughter. "Ms. Maddox, we will be giving a faculty recital at the end of the month. You'll be getting an e-mail but I do hope you'll participate."

"I'd be happy to," I said. "Thank you for thinking of me."

Kent snorted. "You've got this place in an uproar." He forced a smile and lightened his tone. "It would be a crime if you weren't able to perform for us. I'll send you the details by the end of the week." He nodded and continued down the hallway.

Ms. Ellsworth cleared her throat. "Well. Kent is new on the faculty this year. He spent some time out in your stomping grounds, actually. I'm sure you'll have plenty in common."

I wouldn't count on it, I thought. I had Clammy Man's number. He probably had a beef with musicians able to make a living in New York. I'd met scores of people just like him over the years. Kent was the embodiment of why I counted so few people as trusted friends. Jealousy became tiresome to me sometime in the mid-eighties and I stopped making an effort to get past it in my personal relationships. Richard, for example, nursed his own slew of character flaws but jealousy was not one of them. So even with a divorce under our belts, he'd made the friendship cut when so many had not.

Ms. Ellsworth scurried a few paces ahead of me. "Your office is the next door on the left." She unlocked a door with one small rectangular window and gestured for me to enter first.

The room was quite humble but I liked it instantly. I could smell fresh paint, the walls crisp white and unmarred by scuffs or dirt left by the previous occupant. A black baby grand sat at an angle, and a file cabinet, small desk, and chair filled the rest of the space. I walked to the piano and played the first few bars of a Bach minuet. Not the best touch, but it was in tune and had a pleasing, mellow sound. The wall opposite the door boasted a huge window of leaded glass. I walked to it and gathered in my view. The window faced a large lawn broken only by statuesque trees, their branches bare and trembling in the wind. Students crisscrossed the lawn in geometric patterns made by wide sidewalks that stretched like pulled taffy from all corners of the quad. The Kjellman building was one of eight or so that faced this open space, each of them constructed of pale limestone with slate shingles.

Ms. Ellsworth joined me at the window. "Pity you weren't here in fall," she said with a sigh. "Our ivy turns the most glorious red." She pointed to some bare veins of ivy crawling along the top of my window. "Looks like it would have framed your view."

I smiled at her. "As a college *should* look."

Her eyes brightened. "Why, yes. That's what we like to say."

I'd read it in the brochure and suspected it to be misguided self-congratulation at best. But my view from the second floor, even in the bleak midwinter, suggested Moravia's marketing team might have had it right.

A sharp knock sounded on the open door. We turned.

"Mallory!" Ms. Ellsworth hurried over to the girl standing in the threshold.

The girl smiled and I recognized her as the eye-rolling alto. She walked to me and extended her hand. Her smile was syrupy sweet. "Hello, Ms. Maddox. I'm Mallory Knight. I'll be your student assistant."

I took Mallory's hand and shook firmly. "It's a pleasure to meet you, Mallory. I saw you in rehearsal." I raised one eyebrow. "Alto, am I correct?"

She blinked once, kept smiling. "Yes, that's right. You have a good memory."

"Yes, I do," I said, nodding slowly and returning her high wattage grin.

"Mallory is one of our top students," Ms. Ellsworth said. She draped one arm behind the girl and squeezed her petite shoulders. "She sings in the concert choir, plays viola in the orchestra, and still finds time to maintain a 4.0 grade point average. We knew she'd be perfect for this *special* assignment." Ms. Ellsworth drew out the pronunciation of the word, saying *"spay*-shell" with another squeeze to Mallory's shoulders.

Mallory stood straighter. "Just let me know how I can help." She laid an index card with neat handwriting on the desk. "This is my phone number and e-mail address. I've also left my class schedule so you know when I'm available. I'll come by Monday morning after orchestra to see how your first day is going." She grinned. "We hope you find our humble Moravia to be full of surprises."

"I'm sure I will," I said. I put an arm around Mallory and Ms. Ellsworth and moved toward the door. "If you'll excuse me, ladies, I'll just take a moment to get settled."

They walked through the door single file and turned to face me from the hallway. I stood with a hand on the door handle, waving with the other. "Thanks for all your help. See you soon." Ms. Ellsworth looked a bit befuddled at the abrupt good-bye, but I shut the door and walked to the piano bench. I leaned both arms on the music stand and let my head rest on the black wood. I turned my face toward the window and listened to brittle tree branches pester the glass.

So this was it, I thought. Home away from home. Inappropriately affectionate conductor, intimidated baritone, and snippy assistant. All in all, I had to admit, not much different from a morning in New York.

9

First Impressions

I stayed on campus all day. First priority was to collect office essentials. While I would have preferred a bit of monetary help from the department (a fabric chair would have warmed things up, as would a cappuccino maker), Ms. Ellsworth assured me I was on my own for any redecorating, so I made do. I considered calling Mallory back and putting that argyle vest to work, but having to find everything on my own did allow me to see campus. I checked out a CD player from a mullet-sporting audiovisual man named Dax. Dax didn't make eye contact with me once during our exchange, but these people held the keys to the universe in a place like Moravia, so I shut my mouth. Besides, I'd hardly be pleasant either were I to dwell in a shabby office deep within the bowels of the science building.

The beginnings of an in-office CD collection came from the music library on the first floor of Kjellman. Many of the students from concert choir were huddled in and around four rows of listening carrels, large black headphones covering their ears as they practiced their conducting, took notes on Wagner and Bernstein, and hummed along to Mozart. A group of gregarious vocal performance types waved heartily at me and I smiled. A fascinating world, this petri dish of musical education, overrun with neglected hairstyles and bad shoes. I remembered being poor but certainly I hadn't looked *that* fashion-anemic.

A trip to the campus bookstore landed me with two posters for the bare walls: an early Chagall and a cityscape by O'Keeffe that made me nostalgic for buildings that could block the sky. I added to my purchases a bag of dark chocolate (domestic but still palatable), a Moravia College coffee mug, and a small plant that the checkout girl assured me could survive many weeks of neglect before needing resuscitation.

By the end of the afternoon, I'd also happened upon a cavernous and greasy cafeteria that I vowed to avoid at all costs, a small café to provide nourishment for those of us not interested in heart disease, and the campus mail drop. My overall impression of the students was favorable. Most were very friendly, so much so that in New York, they would make people nervous. But here, friendly seemed to be the norm. An abundance of smiles and affable greetings occurred on the sidewalks, even in the face of bitter winter cold.

I'm afraid I simply couldn't reciprocate the chipper attitude; it took me awhile to even realize people kept saying hello to *me*. Perhaps when the weather warmed I'd be better disposed to banter out in the elements.

♪

"How was your first day?" Ms. Ellsworth locked the office door behind her and walked with me to the front doors.

"Fine," I said. Trying to be nice to so many foreign people in one day had worn me out, and I was dreading the long ride out to the farm. I didn't know how long I could listen to stories of wallpaper before my tongue rebelled. I patted my iPod, nestled deep within the pocket of my coat and longed for a technological escape route. "Thank you for offering to drive me home this evening, but what will we do until I get a room at the hotel? I'd assumed I could walk from the rental house, but since that fell through—" I stopped talking as we were assaulted by a gust of painfully cold air. I could feel the small bit of moisture on my eyelashes freeze as we toddled out into the dark. Neither of us spoke again until we were both settled, panting and red-nosed, in Ellsworth's blue Camry.

Ms. Ellsworth started the engine and set about scraping her windows. I shivered in the front seat, watching her and longing for a cab, or even the subway. Anonymous travel had so many merits, a significant one being I never had to sit freezing while a vehicle warmed its frozen self to functioning.

Ellsworth jumped back into the car. "Good gracious," she said, rubbing her hands together. "It's a cold one!"

"So about my transportation to and from campus," I said.

"Yes, right. We have located a lovely little Honda Civic for you. A professor emeritus, Dr. Wheatley, spends her winters in Australia studying aboriginal music. She plays a mean didgeridoo herself. Are you fond of the didgeridoo?" She hunched over her fleece-covered steering wheel as we crawled past student housing and into town.

"Not exactly." I fingered my iPod and wished for this conversation to be over. "And I don't remember how to drive."

She laughed. "Oh, you're a hoot. It's only been a few days! But it is a five-speed, so that might take some getting used to."

"Ms. Ellsworth, most New Yorkers don't drive. Many don't ever get a license. It's simply not feasible for everyone to have their own gas-guzzling pickup or SUV on the crowded streets of Manhattan."

Ms. Ellsworth sniffed. Surely she wasn't offended by SUV bashing. She was driving a Camry, for the love.

I continued. "I do, in fact, know *how* to drive because I grew up in Connecticut and got my license during high school. But then I went to college, moved to New York, and never had the need to renew it. So," I said, sighing, "I'm trying to tell you that I appreciate the didgeridoo player's Honda, but I won't be able to use it."

"I see," Ms. Ellsworth said, nodding slowly. She turned at the feed store and we picked up speed on the dark highway. A semitruck passed us. The Camry trembled in its wake.

We were silent for a few moments before I heard the muffled ring of my cell phone. I fished it out of my bag and answered.

"Hello." It sounded more like a statement than a question.

"Sadie, it's Avi."

"Hi," I said, rubbing my temples. I hoped my headache wouldn't blossom into a full-blown migraine before I could get to my Excedrin caplets up in the Hartleys' attic.

"You sound exhausted, love. Long day?"

"Just tell me if you've found a place," I snapped.

"Touchy, touchy," he said. His voice became muffled. "Sorry about that," he said. "Had to pay my cabbie."

"Must be nice," I mumbled, slumped into my seat. Total blackness barred any view outside my window, but I had a good inkling what I would have seen anyway.

Avi went into professional mode. "I'll be brief. There are no hotel rooms available in Maplewood until after spring break. In fact, there are no hotel rooms within a sixty mile radius that are either (a) habitable by humans or (b) equipped with modern amenities such as an ice machine or cable TV, and certainly not that newfangled Internet Al Gore invented."

I groaned. Ms. Ellsworth looked nervous.

"So, my dear," Avi said, "let's talk about how bad this really is. Is the attic family dreadful?"

"No," I said reluctantly.

"I talked with that secretary at the music department. She's an interesting bird."

"Correct," I said, glancing at Ellsworth. She sat with inappropriately erect posture, readying herself for the big event: the one left-hand turn on the highway before reaching the Hartley place.

"Are you *with* her?" Avi asked in a loud whisper.

"Yes."

"I see. Should I call back?"

I sighed. "No. I give up for now. I'll call you if the need arises."

"I made a reservation for you at the Maplewood Inn starting March twenty-third, and ending the day after graduation."

"Sublime. I'll be waiting with great anticipation."

"You're a champ, Sadie. Seriously. You're like a pioneer woman."

"Interestingly enough, that was never one of my goals in life."

He laughed. "Par for the course in this business, love. I'll call you in a few days. Keep that beautifully sculpted chin up."

I clicked the phone shut. Ellsworth inched the car to a stop by the Hartleys' side door.

"Ms. Maddox," she said, "now, I don't want you to worry for one minute about the transportation issue." She reached over to pat my knee. "I'll be using my noggin all weekend to come to the best solution I can."

My confidence did not soar. "Call me with any news," I said as I let myself out. I trudged up the side steps, tired to the bone and hungry for Excedrin.

"Hey, there," Jayne said as I stepped inside the kitchen. She stood at the sink, washing a colander. "How was your first day?" Her smile was warm, and I tried my best to thaw my chilly manners.

"Long," I said. "I'm heading to bed early."

"Don't you want some dinner?" she asked. She pulled a plate from the fridge. "We ate early but I saved some chicken pot pie for you. Homemade bread, my grandma's cranberry relish."

"Thank you, Jayne." I kept walking toward the stairs. "You're very sweet. But I have a killer headache. If I wake hungry, I'll come heat it up myself." *Drugs, drugs, drugs,* my head screamed. I massaged my forehead as I walked.

"Okay," Jayne said, sounding deflated. "I hope you feel better."

I was halfway up the first set of stairs before I voiced my agreement. "Me too."

The next morning dawned a pale violet. I'd slept straight through the night, at some point tossing my velvet eye mask off the bed. It dangled from the chair by the window. The air was still breathtakingly cold, but the light that suffused the room made it feel warmer than it had the previous day. I could hear the occasional voice of a child downstairs, which was much less disturbing when mingled with the smell of breakfast. My stomach roared an insistent order for whatever was in process in the kitchen. I threw on a velour zip-up and matching pants and headed down the attic stairs.

"Morning, Miss Sadie!" Drew trumpeted.

"Morning, Misadie!" Joel mimicked. The boys crouched over a play train on their bedroom floor. They were still wearing their pajamas, though Drew had added a Daniel Boone cap to his ensemble.

"Wanna play with our trains? *Choo chooooo!*" Drew's train whistle was only slightly less piercing than a high C shrieked by my former, perpetually sharp, understudy named Astrid.

"Maybe I can play with you later," I said. Maybe if your parents are inexplicably detained for hours and there is no other recourse but to play with you and your trains. Maybe then.

"My turn with Percy!" Joel said, grabbing a piece of the train from Drew.

"Mommy!" Drew yelled downstairs.

"*Shhhh!*" Jayne took the stairs two at a time and didn't notice me until she reached the top. She sighed. "I'm sorry. Did they wake you?"

"Not at all," I said. "I slept very well, thank you."

She turned to the boys. "You two get along, all right? Share the trains or we put them away." Jayne steered me toward the stairs. "I hope you're hungry this time. I have a weekend breakfast ready downstairs."

"A weekend breakfast?"

"Just means I don't have to rush Drew off to school and can make something more involved than cereal and a banana."

I breathed deeply. "I smell bacon, pancakes, or maybe French toast …"

Jayne led me downstairs and into the kitchen. "Yes on the bacon and on the French toast. Care for some coffee?"

"With cream, please," I said, and sat down at the table. Jayne set a steaming cup in front of me and a plate heaped with food. The coffee was a bit weak and the French toast soggy. But I was famished and had little room to be picky. Not exactly a plethora of culinary options in the middle of a field. Plus, the bacon was hickory smoked and very crisp, the way God intended. I did not mourn the loss of Wilbur or whichever Hartley animal had been sacrificed for my enjoyment.

I finished my breakfast and sat drinking the rest of the coffee, watching Jayne. Her multitasking skills were borderline miraculous. She washed a dirty pan, answered the phone, and kept up a constant stream of entertaining kitchen implements for Emmalie, who sat at her mother's feet. She did all this while monitoring my emptying coffee cup and coming to offer more. I shook my head and she soon signed off on her telephone call.

"I admire you," I said. "You juggle more in the space of ten minutes than I do in an entire day."

She shook her head, a small smile playing on her lips. "I don't believe that for one minute. You don't become famous by sitting around." She glanced at me, her face apologetic. "Not that I would know anything about being famous, I just meant—"

I held up my hand. "No need for qualifiers. And I'm only famous among people who listen to classical music, a number that appears to need some boosting these days."

Jayne was quiet for a moment, running a dishtowel around an already-dry pot. "Is that why you had to come to Maplewood?"

We heard the front door slam shut and two men laughing.

Jayne slid the clean pot into a drawer by the stove. "The men are back."

The men? Plural?

Jayne called, "Coffee's hot in the kitchen." The baby was suddenly in motion and within seconds had crawled the length of the kitchen and crossed into the dining room.

"Hey, baby girl." I heard Cal's voice just before he entered the kitchen. Right behind him, carrying the giggling Emmalie in his arms, was a tall man with cocoa-colored hair and dark blue eyes that matched those of the baby he hugged.

"Hi," Cal said, leaning over to kiss Jayne.

"We need some introductions," Jayne said. She reached behind Cal to retrieve two more coffee cups.

Cal turned to me. "Morning," he said with a slight nod. "Sadie Maddox, this is my brother, Macalester Hartley."

The tall man moved forward, Emmalie clinging to his neck. He smiled warmly and offered his hand. "Call me Mac."

"Hello, Mac. I'm Sadie." I stayed seated, a fresh horror spreading over me at my lack of makeup, de-greased hair, and supportive brassiere. My smile was tight-lipped. No need to add foul breath leakage to the equation.

"I hear you're quite the singer," Mac said, taking the seat across from me at the kitchen table. "Thank you, Jaynie," he said when she set down a cup of coffee and a little pitcher of milk.

I watched him splash a bit of white into his cup. "I suppose it depends on your preference," I said, wishing I could slap my cheeks for instant color. Honestly, what made me think I could eat my breakfast in solitude as was my normal habit? At the very least I could have used a bronzer ...

"*My* musical preference?" Mac said.

Cal snickered from his post by the open fridge.

"Jaynie, why don't you tell this lovely lady about the musical preferences of the Hartley family?"

Jayne took the baby from Mac's lap, as Emmalie was dangerously curious about his steaming cup of coffee. "Well," she said slowly, "you should know, Sadie. Our Mac is a bit of a local celebrity himself."

"Is that right? Do you sing, Mac?"

"Oh, no," he said, shaking his head and laughing. "I wouldn't wish that on any number of people." He took a long swig of coffee and set down his half-drained cup. "Jaynie is exaggerating about my celebrity status, but I am a big fan of line dancing, the two-step ... anything to country music." He watched my face, one side of his mouth pulled up into a smile. Beautiful, white, even teeth, I had to admit.

"That's wonderful," I said, an achingly false note in my voice. "There's room enough for many types of music in the world. What's important is that you remain open to new kinds of music, no matter what prejudices you may have." I might as well have taken out a lighter and swayed with my eyes shut.

Mac raised his eyebrows and nodded slowly. "I see. That's very diplomatic of you, Ms. Maddox." He cupped two large hands around his mug and leaned forward in his chair. "Have you been line dancing, then?"

I choked on my last sip. After a deliberate swallow, I said, "No, *um*, no. I've heard of it, but I wouldn't know where to start." I shook my head. "Besides, I'm not sure there are venues for that sort of thing in New York."

Mac leaned back in his chair, looking smug. "Crying shame. Well, you'll have to give it a try before you leave us."

I slumped down farther into my chair, wishing I had help with the sag factor. Velour was no respecter of cup size. "I don't think so, but thank you."

"Wait a minute now," Mac said. "Didn't you just preach to me about being open to new kinds of music?"

"Mac," Jayne said. She pushed him playfully but scolded, "Don't be a pest."

I lifted my chin, concealer-free though it was. "I wouldn't consider that preaching. And I was intending that to mean perhaps *you* should look beyond your heartbreakin', knee-slappin', hard-drinkin' repertoire to consider something more high-minded."

Jayne stopped clearing the table and stared. Cal stopped tickling the baby and stood still.

Mac slowly nodded his head, eyeing me with his dark blues. "Well," he said, and stood. "I surely didn't mean to offend. It was a pleasure to meet you, Sadie Maddox. I'm sure we'll see each other again soon, though apparently not on the dance floor." He winked but no smile made it past those teeth. "Cal, Jaynie, we'll see you." He kissed the baby on the top of her head. "Bye now, sweet girl." One more nod to me and he was out the door.

I sat in the kitchen for a few silent moments before thanking Jayne for the breakfast and heading upstairs.

What a pain in the rear, I thought, mulling over the conversation with Mac. Typical insecure male—can dish it out freely but can't take it when a woman stands up to all his hyperbole. I sneaked by the boys' room unnoticed, grateful not to engage in a discussion on the finer points of railroad transportation. Back in my attic, I went straight to the bathroom and started the shower. I docked my iPod on its new little speaker, a consolation gift from Avi before I left. I scrolled through the playlists. "Pre-Mozart Orchestral … Bach … German Art Song … Italian Art Song … Favorite Mezzo Arias …" *All right,* I thought, *so there is somewhat of an overrepresentation of one kind of music.* But it's my job. What I listen to is like market research.

I stepped into the shower and sang along to Kiri Te Kenawa's "O Mio Babbino Caro" full voice.

10

We Gather Together

The Hartleys attended Calvary Baptist Church on the west side of town. The building was long and flat, white with a corrugated green metal roof that Cal said made snow removal a breeze. I wasn't entirely sure what that meant but tried to act like I did.

Per the boys' request and in a moment of goodwill toward their long-suffering mother, who'd already settled six disputes between the front door and the car, I'd sandwiched myself between Drew and Joel in the back seat. Just as we pulled up to the church in the minivan, my phone rang within my purse, which I'd left near the front of the car.

"Would you mind answering that, Jayne?" I asked,

not wanting to risk bodily harm by dislodging myself too abruptly.

"Hello, this is Sadie Maddox's phone," Jayne said, giving me a wide smile and a thumbs-up from the front seat.

"Jayne Hartley," she said shyly and then laughed. And blushed.

Must be Richard.

Cal pulled into a parking space and cut the engine. The baby started crying and Jayne bolted out of the car, one hand covering her exposed ear to hear better.

I rolled my eyes. A thousand miles away and over a wireless network—and Richard was still charming.

"Come on, boys," Cal said as both side doors rolled open. "Drew, wait for Miss Sadie and then help unbuckle your brother."

I pulled myself up and walked folded over like an accordion toward the side door. One endures a great lack of dignity when living with small children.

Jayne was giggling into the phone. "That sounds nice," she said. "I will. Okay. Good-bye." She clicked my phone shut and stood smiling to herself until she saw me standing next to her. "Oh, sorry. Here." She handed me my phone. "That was Richard," she said as if they'd just returned from an extended vacation to the south of France. "He says he'll call later." She took Joel's hand and we started toward the front doors of the church.

I turned my ringer off and let the phone drop into my purse. New pointy-toed stiletto boots gave me an incentive to walk more slowly than normal. Jayne forced Joel to slow his pace to match mine.

She lowered her voice a notch. "So, is he your boyfriend?"

"Richard?" I asked. "Goodness, no. We tried that years ago with disastrous results." A man standing at the front door offered me a church bulletin. "In another life," I said to Jayne as we entered the foyer, "Richard and I were married."

Jayne's eyebrows shot up into her bangs but she didn't have a chance to respond.

"Jaynie!" A plump woman glided toward us. She wore a zebra print turtleneck sweater and a long black skirt. "Helloooo," she said in a lilting, breathy voice. "You must be Sadie Maddox." She scrunched up her nose and covered one of my hands in both of her own. "I'm just deeee-lighted to meet you. I'm Norma Michaels, church pianist." Another nose scrunch.

"Hello, Norma," I said, gently withdrawing my hand from its moist cocoon. "Are you playing in today's service?"

"Oh, yes, of course," she said, glancing at the wall clock in the foyer. "In fact, I'd better skedaddle. I'm sure we'll see a *lot* of each other, Ms. Maddox. We music types tend to flock together." She let out a fluttering laugh that made Joel jump, and then she disappeared through the sanctuary doors.

"Go on in," Jayne said. Joel was tugging her toward the Sunday school classrooms. "Cal and I will find you."

Only a few open chairs remained in the sanctuary. No pews in the church, just chairs upholstered in the same green as the roof. I found a spattering of open seating near the back and kept an eye out for my hosts. In the meantime, Norma sat at a crotchety-sounding baby grand off to one side of the stage. Whatever she lacked in musicality, Norma made up for in body movement. She lifted, she swirled, she closed her eyes and furrowed her brow. A captivating rendition of "Just A Closer Walk With Thee" rang through the sanctuary but probably not in the way the composer intended.

Just as the pastor ascended the steps to the pulpit, Jayne scooted in next to me. Cal slid in and put his arm around her while Mac took the seat on the aisle. We glanced at each other. I quickly returned my gaze to the pulpit.

The pastor, a man with a kind face and horrible shoes, welcomed us to Calvary Baptist and soon gave it over to Norma, who led us in a chorus from the piano. I wasn't familiar with the song so I didn't sing, but Norma was woman enough for us both.

After a lengthy sermon accompanied by an onslaught of PowerPoint slides, we sang a final hymn, "Blessed Assurance," and were dismissed. Cal and Jayne beelined to pick up their children and I was left with Mac.

"How are you, Mac?" I asked, my countenance reflecting the serene and open-minded person I was.

"Very fine, thank you, Ms. Maddox."

"You should call me Sadie."

"All right. How are you, Sadie?" He waved at some people across the lobby and had not yet looked me in the eye.

"Fine," I said, bored already with this man. "Enjoying a warm welcome from the people of Maplewood."

Out of the corner of my eye I thought I saw him wince. He chewed vigorously on his gum for a moment and looked ready to respond when I saw a flash of zebra coming for us.

"Mac," Norma said, her breathy voice dropping an octave. She pulled herself up to her full height. "It's good to see you."

Mac cleared his throat. "Good to see you, too, Norma. I'd like you to meet a friend of mine."

A friend now? I shot him a quizzical look, which he ignored.

"Oh, we've met," Norma said, laying a hand on Mac's arm. He shifted slightly and her hand fell to her side. "Ms. Maddox," Norma turned to me, "I hope you enjoyed the music." Norma shrugged her shoulders like we were sorority sisters about to dish.

"I certainly did," I said. No reason to ruin this woman's life. "You play beautifully."

Mac coughed and then became enthralled with something on the ground by his cowboy boot.

"Perhaps you'll be willing to bless us with a song or two while you're here?" Norma's eyes grew wide. She had mastered the art of eye shadow layering. At close proximity, I could count four different shades of purple.

"I'd be happy to," I said. "Let me get settled in and we'll talk."

She clapped her hands. The zebras trembled. "Wonderful! Isn't that wonderful, Mac?" She looked up at him with doe eyes but he was looking at me.

"I'll look forward to it," he said. Then he nodded. "Ladies, have a good Sabbath." Off he strolled, shaking the hands of people all along his path to the exit.

Norma watched him and sighed.

I broke into her reverie of well-tailored jeans.

"Lovely meeting you, Norma," I said. I thought about offering to put in a good word to her line-dancing crush but was sure I'd be of no help. Better for a lady to fight that battle on her own, animal print and eye shadow at the ready.

♪

Monday morning I was downstairs early. Ms. Ellsworth had promised to be at the Hartleys at 7:30, but I was waiting at the window by 7:15. I tried busying myself with a score Avi had sent that weekend—I was planning to fly back during Moravia's spring break to perform a chamber concert at St. Bart's. I'd performed all the pieces before, but I opened the Handel score anyway to pass the minutes before the Camry pulled up.

At 7:31, a black pickup truck rumbled slowly down the gravel drive. I squinted my eyes through the darkness, trying to focus on the driver who sat shrouded in the glare of headlights. The truck came to a stop and Mac stepped out. He walked briskly to the front door and opened it without knocking. I watched him shake the cold off his shoulders. He looked around and realized I was by the front bay window.

"Ready?" he asked.

I shook my head, confused. "For what?"

"I'm your ride."

"Thanks, but Ms. Ellsworth will be here any minute." I turned back to my score.

Mac crossed his arms over a fleece-lined jean jacket.

He said, "Miranda called me last night. I'm taking over as chauffeur for the famous lady." He walked over to me and took my score, tossed it into my bag and offered his hand.

I stood on my own. "You're a bit pushy, aren't you?" I tugged hard at my scarf, cinching it too tightly around my neck.

He smiled, already chewing fluorescent green gum like cud at this fragile hour. He opened the front door and held it for me to pass through.

I kept my face burrowed into my scarf. The sun peeked over the horizon with a disheartening lack of confidence. Mac strode ahead of me to the passenger side and opened the door.

"What is it with Iowan men and pickups?" I muttered. "Ghastly things, probably an effort to overcompensate …" I took his hand and heaved myself up into the cab. I settled into the seat and let Mac close the door. He shook his head as he rounded in front of the headlights.

Mac revved the engine once and U-turned back toward the driveway. I could see Jayne waving from the kitchen door, not appearing one bit surprised that Mac was behind the wheel instead of Ms. Ellsworth. *No matter,* I thought, pulling my iPod out of my coat pocket. Pickup or Camry made no difference to me, as I planned on keeping to myself during the commute into Maplewood.

I tucked in one earphone and turned to Mac. "I don't wish to offend you, but I'll be using drive time as work time."

Mac nodded once. "Fine. I like to prepare for my day as well."

"What is it you do?"

His face reflected the glow of dashboard lights. "Well, Miss Sadie, I'm willing to guess you've never met someone who has my job."

I scrolled on my iPod to the piece Avi had sent. "I'm sure you're right, Mr. Hartley. I'd never met a pig farmer before coming to Maplewood and now I'm sharing Cheerios with one."

Mac chuckled. "I'm a large animal veterinarian."

I snapped to attention. "What, exactly, does that mean?"

"I take care of farm animals. Cattle, horses, sheep, pigs. Immunizations, bone setting, putting animals down when needed. We're coming up on spring, which will be busy with all the castrating." He looked at me out of the corner of his eye.

"Lovely," I said. "You know how to castrate large animals."

"Not a lot of guys like me running around New York City, I imagine." He winked at me.

I sighed. "You are correct. Castration is not a hot topic in Manhattan, at least not in the literal sense." I popped in the other earphone and pushed play for the Handel. I closed my eyes and listened until the truck rolled to a stop in front of Kjellman. I reached for the door handle, but Mac was already out of the cab. He opened my door and helped me down.

"Thank you," I said, noting flecks of green in his blue eyes.

"You're welcome." He looked down at me, face as serious as the grave but his eyes dancing with laughter. "I don't wish to offend, but we pickup types prefer a lady to sit tight until we can open her door. Hope that's not too prehistoric for you."

I raised my chin slightly. "Of course not," I said and adjusted my bag strap on my shoulder. "It's an admirable gesture, though certainly not necessary."

He shoved his hands into his coat pockets and grinned. "You don't like depending on people, do you?"

A formidable wind sucked the air right out of my lungs. "You," I sputtered, "don't know me well enough to make that comment. See you this evening." I snapped my gaze away from his grin and strode up to the double doors. I didn't know what was worse: living in Iowa in the winter or having to share a small, enclosed space with a psychoanalyzing castration expert. I shivered as I walked down the tiled hallway, shaking off the cold for my first day of school.

Andante

"Next week the Copland," I said.

"Thank you, Ms. Maddox," James said. Five weeks into the semester and with a burgeoning studio of students, James was one of my favorites. He wasn't a music major, which explained why he was so self-assured. James came from a long line of athletes, and Moravia paid his tuition in exchange for services on the basketball court. Music, he'd told me, was his guilty pleasure. A deep, easy baritone came naturally to James. And though I wouldn't have predicted it judging by those horrible nylon shorts hanging well below his knees in all kinds of weather, James had a poet's appreciation of language.

He shoved his notebook and *lieder* into a fraying backpack. Long, dark curls fell into his eyes. He pulled a strand behind an ear and straightened to his full six feet, six inches. He looked down at me wide-eyed and said, "Ms. Maddox, you were amazing in the faculty recital. My music friends can't stop talking about it."

"You're too kind, James," I said. The truth was that I'd forgotten about the recital until a few days before, when the insecure Norwegian had sent me a reminder e-mail. I'd chosen two tried and true encore arias and had met only once with the pianist. The reception, particularly from the students, had been very warm. I couldn't remember the last time I'd received such unfettered and thunderous applause. Too bad no one from the *Times* had been there to review.

"Dude, I know I'm a baritone, but I'd kill to have your pipes. Even as a guy." James looked mildly confused by his own reasoning.

I arched one eyebrow. "James, I'm sure there are counselors on campus who can help you work through any gender issues you have."

"Okay. All right." His eyes twinkled. "I can take the sass. 'Gender issues …'" He shook his head of curls in mock disapproval. "You're not exactly the typical professor, are you?"

I sniffed. "Not by a long shot. Practice hard and I'll see you next week."

He grinned and ambled out the door. I propped it open behind him and looked down the hall. Mallory Knight, my elusive student assistant, held the next slot and was late yet again. Her initial Little Miss Can't-Do-Wrong impersonation with the neatly inked index card and syrupy smiles had been solely for the benefit of Ellsworth. I'd seen very little initiative from the girl since. Once, after two phone messages and three e-mails, I'd gotten her to photocopy some materials for my students. But the effort involved in coercing work out of her had prevented me from enlisting Mallory's services again. I'd thought about broaching the topic with Ellsworth but decided I'd rather get my own coffee and Xerox copies if I could avoid Mallory's incompetence and snobbery in one fell swoop.

I sighed to think of the half hour before me and headed back into my office. The view outside my window was pristinely white. We were well into February and had been hit by a series of snowstorms in the previous weeks. I'd come to prefer snow to the gray. Delicate white lines outlined the branches arching past my window. I watched a group of boys pelt each other with snowballs. A passerby ducked to avoid being hit.

"Sorry I'm late," Mallory said letting the door shut with a bang.

I turned from the window.

Mallory flopped down with a thud on a chair by the piano, cheeks flushed and eyes bright.

"It's fine," I said slowly, "though you'll end up with a shorter lesson."

"Oh, well," she said, smiling sweetly. "My loss, then."

I sat at the piano. "Mallory, do you have a problem with being late to other classes as well?" I cringed even as the words came out of my mouth.

Her eyes widened. "You know what, Ms. Maddox? Now that you say it, I don't think I do. You're the *only one* I'm consistently late for." She shook her head in bewilderment.

I studied her a moment. Chocolate-colored hair cut just above the shoulders so that it swung when she walked. Long lean legs, showcased today in an A-line skirt and tall boots. Olive skin, brown eyes, full lips, and straight teeth that matched the white Peter Pan collar peeking out from the top of a fitted sweater. Most of my students at Moravia were like James, sweet, compliant, deferential to the fact that I knew far more than they did about most things. But this tart before me was a test of my goodwill.

"Shall we then?" I said briskly. "Take out the Mozart."

She riffled through a small stack of music.

If she couldn't bring herself to be civil, I thought as I waited, I'd just watch her flounder until forced to ask for my help. During our lessons in weeks prior, Mallory had fumbled through her assignments, clearly having neglected the many practice rooms in Kjellman. I knew she was double majoring in voice and viola performance, something I thought absolutely ludicrous and an indulgence that would be openly mocked at more prominent conservatories. Even with divided attention and demands on her time, or perhaps because of them, I expected her to bring her absolute best to my office. I'd been promised the cream of the vocal performance crop, and she was failing miserably.

I opened my score, glanced over the page, and couldn't help but smile. Kind-hearted educators probably ached in the face of their students crashing and burning, but I knew as I looked over this particular aria that a few moments of revenge were to be mine. This piece was a killer, with an Italian text that demanded an emotional maturity I was sure she didn't have. She'd picked the piece herself, though, and had lobbied for her readiness. I plunked out a few chords to set her up for the recitative and brought her in with a nod.

The beginning measures were a train wreck. Her eyes were glued to the score, she was unsure of the Italian pronunciation, and she had all the grace of a box turtle as she moved with the music. In my benevolence, I did not roll my eyes. As the recit drew to a close, I decided to let her continue into the aria, knowing within a few phrases of the coloratura, she'd bow out on her own.

Mallory put down her score and stepped away from it slightly. She drew in a slow breath from the diaphragm and began. I went from catty indifference to disbelief as my mouth hung open. Her phrases became languid and sweet, air moving through each line with energy and life. Her eyes came alive, sparking with the text as she described the betrayal of a lover. The diction was still shaky in parts, but as I finished the final few measures of accompaniment, I was weak from emotional involvement in her performance.

Silence fell. I looked up from the piano keys. "Mallory," I said, "where has *that* been the last month?"

She shrugged. "I guess I connect with this piece."

I nodded slowly. "It shows. Your lines are like taffy. You draw out emotion in places most singers your age would skip right over. And while I've always thought your tone was pleasant, today it was magnificent." I shook my head, mostly to myself. "I thought you'd fall flat on your face."

Her face hardened instantly. "Why? Because I'm at a no-name college instead of at Juilliard or Eastman?" She started gathering her things even though we still had ten minutes left.

I stood up and put both hands firmly on the top of the piano. "Actually, because you have given me no reason to believe otherwise. Your treatment of me and of the music you've been studying has been, at best, mediocre. But today, for a dramatic change, you were excellent."

She let out a short laugh and tossed her music into a bulging purple backpack. She hefted it onto a bony shoulder and stood in front of me. I saw in her face one of the many reasons I'd never regretted having children, so many of whom end up hating their parents anyway. "Ms. Maddox," she said, "I'm glad you liked me today. But guess what?" She enunciated much more clearly in English than Italian. "I'm only studying with you this semester because my voice teacher requested it of me. She thinks I harbor secret longings for a career in New York, though I've never said anything to that effect. She thinks studying with you will *inspire* me, *motivate* me to want fame like the great Sadie Maddox." She said my name like the words might infect her. "She's wrong. But I'm here anyway. Let's just make the best of it, shall we?"

She turned to go and I put my hand on her shoulder to stop her. "Listen, missy," I said, my voice low. "*I* am the one making concessions here." I could feel my heart pounding and my hands starting to shake. "Do not presume to tell me you're doing me a favor." I stepped between her and the door and looked at her, eye to squinty little coed eye. "Come *every* week with your A game or I'll transfer you right back to Sweetie Pie Voice Teacher who doesn't know New York talent from a cockapoo. Are we agreed?"

For the first time in our relationship, Mallory looked impressed with me.

"Got it," she said, blinking once.

I moved aside and let her leave.

♪

The rumble of Mac's truck filtered through the heavy front doors of Kjellman. I buttoned my coat and pulled on a pair of cinnamon gloves with matching beret. Using all my body weight, I persuaded one of the doors to open and stood for a moment under the roof. The world was awash with lumbering, wet snowflakes that dropped unceremoniously from a milky sky. Mac strode up the walk like it was seventy degrees and sunny instead of fifteen and a personal injury lawyer's dream. He offered me his arm without a word. We moved slowly down the walk, my pointy-toed heels making triangular, sliding tracks in my wake.

"You're not one for practical clothes, are you?" Mac muttered, visibly annoyed with our snail's pace.

"But think of the dividends in how good I look."

Mac grunted, completely missing his opportunity to flatter a woman. I shook my head under the beret. It was no wonder the man was single.

I pulled myself up into the warm cab of Mac's pickup. In the weeks since I'd arrived in Maplewood, I'd become a veritable cowgirl in my ability to scale large vehicles.

Mac threw open his door and shoved the gearshift into reverse in one smooth motion. In the course of our morning and evening commutes, Mac and I had settled into a comfortable arrangement. We'd converse if the mood hit us but did not feel compelled to fill the air with mindless banter. He let me listen to my iPod, make notes to my students or on my scores, and take calls when necessary. I was content to leave him to his brooding silences and to an extent, his country music, as long as the volume didn't interrupt my train of thought.

We crept around the town square, even the snow-adept drivers of Maplewood using extra caution on the roads that evening. I watched the flakes erase the brown of winter, stubborn and still staking its claim at the end of February. A whiny woman on the radio crooned about tight jeans and red lipstick, all the things her man loved.

"When does spring arrive in Iowa?" I asked, watching a woman shuffle down the street clinging to a paper bag of groceries.

Mac shrugged. "Sometimes the beginning of March, usually by the end April."

I sighed. "I don't know how you stand it. Spring can be elusive in New York as well, but at least there are distractions from the dismal weather."

"And what, Sadie Maddox, are your favorite distractions?" He kept his eyes on the road but there was a smile in his voice.

I cleared my throat. "My distractions. *Hmmm.* I love going to dinner with friends, attending concerts, exhibits, galas—"

"Galas?"

"Charity functions, fund-raising balls, black-tie affairs. I like to dress up."

"Wouldn't have guessed that."

"In addition," I said pointedly, "I like to dance. Not the way you do it here, but the old-fashioned way. I like ballroom dancing."

Mac stole a glance at me. "That right?"

I nodded. "It's so elegant. Of course, everything depends on the man. If you have a useless male leading, it's impossible to resurrect a dance from death."

Mac shook his head and chuckled. "Just tell me how you feel, now. Don't be shy."

I laughed, too, and was still smiling when my phone rang. It was Richard.

"Richard, how are you?"

"Fine, darling. You sound bubbly. Smell of manure getting to you?"

"You know, I believe the stench has subsided. Or perhaps I'm more fully evolved than you thought I was."

"So self-evolution is connected to pig droppings?"

"Richard, I'm in great spirits," I continued without pause. "I'm on my way home in a snowstorm but perfectly safe in the hands of Mac Hartley, pickup driver and line dancer extraordinaire."

"Oh, yes, Mac. Of course," Richard said. "Give the guy a slap on the back for me, won't you?"

I pulled the phone away. "Mac, Richard says hello."

Mac nodded curtly and kept his eyes glued to the road.

"Mac says hello, too, Richard. He's busy saving me from a tumble into the ditch." A flock of lights flickered in the distance. Mac slowed the truck and rolled down his window to talk to a state trooper parked on the opposite side of the road.

"Evening, BJ," Mac said, leaning out to shake the trooper's hand. I tuned back into Richard's voice.

"Listen, Sadie, I can't chat long but I wanted you to know I've booked reservations at Deseo for when you're back in March. I thought I'd call ten or so of our closest friends and we'd celebrate your prison break together."

"That sounds lovely," I said, a lightness filling my chest. "Richard, you have no idea how thrilled I am to be coming home." I could smell Deseo's famous *paella* even in Mac's Armor All-ed truck.

"It's a date then," Richard said. "I'll call you later, love. I'm almost to the city. We have rehearsal at seven."

"With whom?" I asked. Rehearsal with anyone familiar with the cultural importance of MoMA sounded exquisite.

"I'm conducting Dvorak's 'New World' and the Sibelius violin concerto this weekend at Carnegie. Moscow Symphony Orchestra is here on tour and Maestro Igor is down with the flu, poor gangly thing. I got the call last night."

"Richard, that's fantastic!" I exclaimed. "What a compliment!"

"I know, I know." Richard couldn't keep the pride out of his voice. "I'm pleased. They might have called sixteen people before they got to me, but at least I was on the list to begin with."

"Congratulations," I said warmly. "I'm so happy for you."

"Thank you, darling. I'll call later and tell you how it went."

He hung up and I snapped the phone shut.

Mac rolled up the window as BJ retreated back to his patrol car. "Richard landed a huge conducting job this weekend," I said aloud. "I'm thrilled for him." I turned to Mac. "It'd be like you getting the chance to, say, treat the president's dog."

Mac let his head roll to the side slowly. He looked at me with bored amusement. "The president's dog is senile and nearly dead. But," he said, shrugging his broad shoulders like a question mark, "if the president needed help birthing his prize heifer, well, then." His grin made something jump in my stomach. "I'd be just the man." He pulled the truck slowly onto the shoulder and turned us back toward town.

"What are you doing? Aren't we going home?" I hadn't intended it, but my voice did rise sharply with my question. I watched *Law and Order,* people. I knew not to let the perp bring you to a second location. Of course, this particular perp had been shuttling me back and forth to work for weeks, but still.

"Road's closed up ahead. A semi lost control and is blocking the highway."

"Oh, dear Lord," I said, exasperated. "This is just one more reason people are meant to live in more populated areas. In New York, for example, we have more than one route home." I sighed.

"You'll be happy to know no one was hurt."

I cleared my throat. "That's good to hear." I shifted in my seat. *I* can *think of others, I* can *think of others,* I thought. That blasted Golden Rule was such an annoyance. "So where are we headed?"

Mac turned into one of the many empty parking

spaces along Main Street. "Dinner. A man's got to eat, even in a snowstorm." He pulled the key from the ignition. "Want to join me?"

I looked ahead of us. A warmly lit café beckoned. I tried not to think of the processed cheese, flavorless meat, and iceberg lettuce that awaited me. We were in the middle of a natural disaster, after all.

"Fine," I said, and waited for Mac to open my door.

12

Local Flavor

A balding man in an apron looked up from his position behind the grill. "Seat yourself, Mac," he called.

"Thanks, Harv." Mac removed his ball cap and turned to me. "Booth in the middle all right?" he asked.

I led the way to the center of a wall of red vinyl booths. Mac hung his cap on a hook perched on the side of our booth. We scooted into seats opposite each other.

"How's it going, Don?" Mac nodded to a man in a nearby table. "Weather cold enough for you?"

Don shook his head. "You know this ain't cold, Mac Hartley. Snowy, yes. A tad inconvenient, maybe. But cold hasn't even knocked on the door." He joined Mac in hearty laughter and turned back to an impossibly large cheeseburger. If Don had asked my opinion, I would have corrected him on both the cold and his choice of nutrition. He had to be weighing in at three bills and yet the artery clogging continued.

"We have some uncharacteristic silence at this table," Mac said, eyebrows raised over his menu. He slid a plastic booklet with a printed cover over to me: *Harvey's Café, Where Friends Meet to Greet and Eat.*

"I'm taking in the ambience," I said, opening my menu. "I'm surprised so many people are out and about."

Mac surveyed the busy dining room. "We're a hearty people, Ms. Maddox." His eyes were nothing but ornery. "You'd probably feel more comfortable in this weather too, if you could stop wearing shoes to break your neck in."

I sighed. "While I'm indebted to your fashion savvy, Mac, I'd prefer a recommendation on what to order." I ran my finger down the list of Harvey's offerings. "I'm seeing an abundance of pork products."

Mac nodded. "Chops are good. Burgers are good. Chicken-fried steak is good."

"Which is it? A chicken or a steak?"

Mac looked confused. "It's a steak. Fried like a chicken." He licked his lips. "Harvey makes a good gravy … Sounds good tonight." He slapped his menu shut and grinned at me. "Why are you wrinkling your nose?"

"I'm still dealing with the fried chicken steak issue."

Mac looked up. "Hey, there. How are you?"

I looked up to see the waitress who'd slapped a couple waters on the table. Mallory Knight met my gaze with wide eyes.

"Ms. Maddox. Hi." She shifted on her feet.

Mac shook his head at me. "You *are* famous, aren't you? And I thought it was all hype."

I shot him a look and was entirely distressed to find him attractive, even as he smirked. I turned quickly back to Mallory. "I didn't know you worked here."

"I didn't know you knew this place existed." She took out her order pad and a pen. "Besides, student assistantships don't really pay a whole lot."

Which is justice, I thought, *since you don't do squat.*

"Mac Hartley," he said, reaching forward to shake Mallory's hand. "I'm Ms. Maddox's private chauffeur."

Mallory's eyebrows shot up. "Are you serious?"

"He most certainly is not," I said, huffy. "Well, he *is* in a sense, but not the way he's making it sound."

Mac winked at our impressionable young waitress. "It's exactly as it sounds, my dear. You appear to know Ms. Sadie well enough to have a good idea of her expectations."

Mallory smiled at Mac and put one hand on her hip. "I do, in fact. She has very, very high expectations." She glanced at me. The sass was back home on her face.

All I need, I thought. Obnoxious and More Obnoxious ganging up on me. I smiled like the gracious Queen Mother. "Speaking of high expectations, I've heard great things about your menu."

Mallory became all business. "Are you ready to order, then?"

"I'll have the pork chop," I said. "If Harvey has a history of overcooking, please encourage him to under- rather than over-. For the sides, I'll have steamed vegetables, no salt, and the homemade roll. Do you have iced tea?"

Mallory was scribbling furiously on her notepad. "Only in the summer," she said, not looking up.

"Then I'll have hot tea with two lemon slices on the side."

"Got all that?" Mac asked, shaking his head at Mallory.

"I sure hope so." She jerked her head at me. "You know about the *expectations*."

"I like this girl," Mac said, ignoring the daggers I sent his way. "Mallory, I'd just like a chicken-fried steak, if you will. Sides of Harvey's famous applesauce and the rolls for dipping. Large chocolate milk with my dinner and coffee after the meal."

"Thanks," Mallory said, tucking the notepad into her apron.

She retreated to the kitchen window and Mac smiled at me. "Don't be grumpy."

I crossed my arms. "I'm not."

"Yes, you are," he said as if he'd pronounced the sky blue. "You take yourself too seriously."

"There you go again," I said, exasperation pouring out of my voice. "Why do you assume the right of telling me about my inner thought life? First, I don't like people taking care of me and now I'm too serious with myself?"

Mac watched me for a moment. "So, am I right?"

"And besides." I lowered my voice. "You don't know her." I narrowed my eyes toward Mallory, who was dressing salads behind a counter. "She seems sweet as sugar right now, but the girl has an issue with authority."

"Ah," he said, nodding slowly. "You see yourself in her."

"You are insane," I sputtered. "I'm taking a walk." I

started to stand, disgusted I'd been coerced into having dinner with that man.

"Now, hold on a minute," Mac said, laying a warm and calloused hand on mine. "Sit down, you crazy woman. You're not going for a walk in a snowstorm. Sit down, now. Come on."

I sat slowly and didn't withdraw my hand, which could, in retrospect, be seen as a sign of weakness.

"Listen," he said, returning his hand to his side of the table. "I didn't mean to offend you. Just rile you up a bit." Blue eyes sparkled as he took a draw of water. "But I'm not sure you're used to people riling you up."

"Not like that," I said, wishing I could give in to my lower lip's desire to jut into a satisfying pout. "Most people save their comments to share with other musicians behind my back."

"Ouch," he said. He leaned back and dangled one arm along the booth behind him.

I shrugged, trying not to notice how nice he looked in a worn old button-down. *Pull yourself together,* I thought, and concentrated on sipping the tea Mallory had set down in front of me. The storm must have been knocking a few loose, for surely Mac had not provoked the change in my heart rate.

We chatted a bit about less threatening things, like the Hartley kids (Mac adored them), the weather (I despised it), and Jayne's pies (shared awe). Mallory approached our table with two plates piled high with food. She set mine down first.

"Pork chop, done to a perfect 160 degrees," she said, "and chicken-fried steak with extra gravy, because Harvey knew you'd want it."

"Good man," Mac said.

"Can I get you two anything else?" Mallory was watching me closely, eyes darting between my eyes and my plate. Had she spit on the chop or something?

"I don't think so, thank you," I said and Mallory took her leave.

"Shall I say grace?" Mac asked, then looked a bit uncomfortable. "Or I could pray silently."

"Let me guess." I tilted my face to one side. "People from New York are godless atheists who think religion is, at best, provincial and at worst, destroying everything from the environment to presidential politics."

Mac looked sheepish. "I'll pray, then." He bowed his head. He waited a moment and then spoke quietly. "Heavenly Father, thank you for this dinner and for your continued provision for us. Please bless the food to our bodies so that we might serve you better. Thank you for Sadie, Lord, and for her willingness to share a meal with me. Bless her with a new sense of your love for her during the time she stays with us in Maplewood. Amen."

I swallowed a lump rising in my throat. Mac took a sip of water but I thought I could see blush creeping into his cheeks. I smiled. "Thank you, Mac. I can't remember the last time someone blessed me."

He busied himself with his napkin and cleared his throat. I steeled myself for a retort, but he said only, "You're welcome." Then, fork in one hand and knife in the other, he flashed a huge grin. "Shall we?"

• • •

"I don't understand it," I said for the second time. We were crawling through the dark and snow toward the Hartley farm, bellies full and bodies warm in the heated truck. "Of course I've had pork chops before, but they didn't taste like *that*."

Mac allowed a smile around his toothpick but kept his eyes on the road.

"And all he used was salt and pepper. No mango coulis, no cilantro-lime marinade … Just salt and pepper." I shook my head, more annoyed than pleased. How much money had I spent during my lifetime on bad pork? And how was it that a town with no working stoplights could instruct me on the finer points of meat preparation?

Mac turned the window defroster up a notch. "I'm glad you liked it, but that Mallory was downright excited."

"She really was," I said, marveling at the second miracle of the evening. "It was as if she took the pork personally. She *smiled* at me on the way out. And it was a real smile, not one of those saccharine ones she usually comes up with."

"It was a good meal," Mac said, and I nodded to my window in assent.

We rode the rest of the way in silence, listening to a deep-voiced man on the radio sing about his favorite beer while Mac tapped his fingers on the steering wheel and hummed along.

13

Snow Day

The next day Moravia cancelled classes. Cal shook his head in disbelief, sure the college had never before closed its doors on account of weather, not during his lifetime, at least. Drew stayed home from school and ran around the house for the first hour crowing about his good fortune. Joel joined in on the crowing though all he would miss that day was a trip to town for groceries. Emmalie looked at me from her high chair, masticating slices of banana placed on her tray with great vigor.

"Emmy," I said to her through the steam rising from my teacup. "You and your mother will need each other for solace in this house." I shook my head. "I shudder to think of the marked increase of testosterone levels over the years."

Jayne laughed and took a sip of orange juice. "Can you imagine junior high?" She rose from the table and kissed Emmy on one of her fat cheeks. "We girls will just need to stick together, right, sweet pea?"

Emmy gurgled through her banana, sending a chunk of it sliding down her bib. I felt proud that the sight didn't make me want to vomit. Maplewood had already been a growth experience, had it not?

"What will you do today, Sadie?" Jayne started in with the paper towel facial she gave Emmy each morning after breakfast.

"I need to practice." I drained the rest of my tea. "My chamber concert in New York is two weeks away and I have to clean up the Handel." I rinsed out the cup by the sink and dried my hands on a red-checked towel.

"We'll leave you alone, then," Jayne said. "I'll do my best to keep the boys quiet. Maybe send them outside to build a snow fort."

I waved away her worry. "When I practice, not even a jackhammer can distract me. Your boys will be fine."

Look at me, I thought as I ascended the stairs to the second floor. *Little Miss Accommodating.* I smiled to myself, smug with my ability to live as the Romans did. Up in the attic, I began vocalizing, starting with simple humming up and down from tonic to dominant. I stretched, I walked, I blew air through my lips like a tired horn player. I even did two sets of ten jumping jacks to get my heart pumping and my body awake. I was forever reminding my students at Moravia that singing was a physical activity. One's entire being had to be engaged because the body *was* the instrument. My favorite voice teacher in undergrad had kept a small trampoline under her baby grand. If my singing was lethargic, my tone uninspired, my breath support desperate, Ms. Groves would haul out the trampoline and watch with a poker face while I jumped. When she was satisfied, I'd hop back off the tramp and sing. Inevitably, my body felt the singer's cherished paradox of being grounded and free at the same time. I didn't have a trampoline in my office at Moravia, but jumping jacks worked and once the weather cooperated, I'd order laps around the quad.

My pitch pipe gave me an F, and I was soon immersed in the Handel. The ornamentation of the second section of the piece had been giving me trouble so I took my time revisiting how I wanted those phrases to sound. During a lull, while I reconsidered a series of breath marks, I heard insistent whispering behind the door at the foot of the stairs.

"But Mommy, why are you sitting on the floor?"

"*Shhh!* I'm listening." Jayne's whisper voice was much more convincing than Drew's.

"Listening to what?" he said in an impatient stage whisper.

"*ShhhHHH!*" Jayne said. "I'm listening to Miss Sadie sing."

"What song is she singing?" Drew said.

Joel piped in. "Is it from VeggieTales?"

"Drew, honey," Jayne said, betraying in her voice her feeling that Drew wasn't such a honey at that moment. "I don't want Miss Sadie to hear us because she's working, so—"

I had crept downstairs and opened the door slowly as she spoke. Jayne looked up, the baby on her lap and both boys standing before her. They looked up at me with solemn eyes, certain of their impending doom at the hands of their mother.

"I'm so sorry," Jayne said, hoisting to her feet, Emmy swaying and clinging to her mom's neck. Jayne tucked a strand of blonde past her reddened cheek. "I was just discussing with the boys how we didn't want to bother you." She shot them a look that made their chins droop.

"Well, I'm here now, so let's try a different approach." I turned to the boys. "Drew and Joel, would you and the girls like to join me upstairs for a short concert?"

Drew snapped his head to attention. "Like with drums?"

Jayne nudged him. "No drums, buddy. Miss Sadie is going to sing for us." She barely waited for me to clear the first stair before jumping in line behind me. The baby squealed as Jayne ascended to the top. The boys straggled along behind, disappointed like so many others that I couldn't accompany myself on drums or electric guitar.

Jayne gathered her children around her, the boys on either side and the baby on her lap.

"Welcome to Hartley Concert Hall," I said in my soap-opera-star voice. "My name is Sadie Maddox and I will be your entertainment for the next few minutes. Sit back, relax, and enjoy the music."

This was where the orchestra should have launched into a sweeping overture, but my resources were limited. I played a lone E on the pitch pipe and began.

The Hartleys were a good audience, at least for the first sixteen measures. Jayne's eyes shone, her back straight as a pin as she watched my every move. The baby bounced up and down and clapped her chubby paws. Drew sat with his skinny legs crossed, slumped with chin in hands and appearing to be comfortable in his pretzel shape as only young children can be. He exhibited the Hartley male eye gene: bottomless blue, wide and watchful. Joel stared at me with the same eyes, only he covered both ears. Full volume classical singing at close range could make a person's eardrums tremble like a brittle November leaf. I was the first to admit that and took no offense at Joel's efforts to drown me out.

Even with their good intentions, however, my audience, only one of whom rose above four feet in height, got weary of the Handel before I reached the second theme. So I capped it off and accepted their applause. Emmalie hadn't stopped clapping from start to finish but the boys took their opportunity to grace me with effusive accolades, including dog sounds and armpit farts. Jayne chastised them as best she could without stopping her own applause.

"That was beautiful," she said, eyes shining. "I've never heard anything like it in my life." She pulled her sweatshirt sleeve over her hand and used it to dab at her eyes. "I mean, we have some CDs of yours, and Cal got me one with Kathleen Battle for my birthday one year, but in person ..." she trailed off, shaking her head. She took a deep breath and smiled shakily. "Would you mind singing one more?"

"I'd love to," I said. *Perhaps Avi was right about this move,* I thought. These people were far more appreciative than any roomful of music snobs back East. At least the culturally poor and needy remembered to say thank you.

As a contrast to the perpetual motion of the Handel, I sang a haunting lullaby by Schumann for the second piece. I kept it in the German, as translating it to English would have been like telling an editor at *Bon Appétit* to dip his sushi in ketchup. Some things are meant to stay true to their original form.

Jayne swayed lightly with Emmy on her lap. The baby plugged in her thumb and hummed a monotone line along with my own. Drew lay down on the hardwood and appeared to be counting the overhead beams. Joel said loudly during the second verse, "But Mom, does she know any VeggieTales songs?"

I finished the piece and received another round of arm flatulence and wild clapping. Jayne stood with Emmy and threw her free arm around my neck. "Thank you," she said into my hair. "I feel like I've seen the best of New York in my own house." She pulled away and started herding the boys toward the stairs.

"Jayne," I said, "wait just a moment, will you?" I raised my eyebrows and looked at the boys.

"Drew and Joel," Jayne said, still looking at me. "Go on downstairs and get out your Lincoln Logs. I'll be down in a minute."

The boys raced for the stairs. "Be careful," Jayne warned as, without care for broken bones, they plummeted down the steep attic staircase. She shuddered as they reached the bottom without incident.

I sat down on the chair by the window and crossed my legs. "Jayne, what are you doing the second weekend in March?"

She looked confused but answered obediently. "*Um,* the usual, I guess." She searched the ceiling for her plans. "Make a pancake breakfast for the kids, do some errands in town, make lunch, make dinner, clean the house. I think there might be a potluck after church Sunday." She looked at me and shrugged. "All that glamour packed into two short days. Can you believe it?" The baby started to fuss and Jayne put her down on the floor. Emmy got up on all fours and crawled directly to the bathroom. Jayne hurried ahead to shut the door. I'd been warned of Emmy's new interest in toilet fishing.

"Come with me to New York."

Jayne stopped with her hand on the bathroom doorknob. She looked at it a moment and then raised her gaze to meet mine. "New York? With you?"

I nodded. "Sure. Cal can take care of the kids for a couple days, can't he?" I wasn't entirely sure this was true but I did my best to sound confident. Lord knew I would run from the room screaming like a little girl if someone asked me to do such a thing.

Jayne bit her bottom lip, looking every bit as uncertain as I felt. She sucked in her breath. "I don't think so, actually. I would fear for their survival."

"What about a nanny? Can you hire someone?"

Jayne looked at me as if I'd abruptly switched to speaking Cantonese.

I tried a different approach. "What about Cal and Mac together? Certainly two intelligent men can take on three children who don't even know their times tables."

"You want me to come to New York City with you? A weekend in New York City?"

This wasn't supposed to be so difficult. "Yes," I

spoke slowly and clearly. "As my guest. You'll only need money for a cheesy souvenir from Empire State." *I can afford it,* I thought. It wasn't as if I'd been a spendthrift out here in the boonies. Other than a modest monthly check made out to the Hartleys, I'd had very few expenses. I could feel the goodwill inside me soaring to new heights. Maybe I was becoming a nice person.

Jayne seemed to emerge out of the cloud. "I'll figure it out. Yes," she said, smiling suddenly, giddily. "I've only ever been to Chicago once in college. And to Branson for our honeymoon." She hurried over and hugged me fiercely. "I'll go. Thank you, Sadie."

I thought she might start crying so I stood. "It's my pleasure," I said. "Now leave me alone so I can get back to work."

Jayne scooped up the baby and went flying down stairs, not a whole lot more safely than the boys, and she was carrying a child to boot. I began the second movement of the Mozart and smiled to myself. *Watch out, New York,* I thought. *Jayne Hartley is in the market for a snow globe.*

14

Start Spreading
the News

By the time plows had cleared the highway the next afternoon, I was regretting my kind gesture. As predicted, Cal put up a bit of a fuss when Jayne told him about the trip. The air at the dinner table that evening was wrought with tension, and my presence didn't help. I endured half my meatloaf before excusing myself to the attic. I gave Jayne a subtle thumbs-up on my way out and she sat up in her chair, eyes glinting with fresh resolve.

I stayed upstairs the entire evening, not wanting to interfere on any progress that might have been made. Cal seemed to be the type of man who wouldn't appreciate my meddling in an argument with his wife. He was also more stubborn than spilled merlot on white silk, so frankly, I wasn't holding out much hope that my impromptu idea would come to fruition.

The next morning the snow had stopped and the sun shone into every cell of the white earth. I stood at my window, wrapped in a quilt and squinting into the bright daylight. I watched as a stream of melting snow made its way down the roof. Mac had been right—March snow was likely in Iowa but at least it had the sense not to overstay its welcome.

I followed my nose downstairs to the pancakes, eggs, and bacon Jayne had whipped up in celebration of Saturday. When I rounded the corner into the kitchen, I was surprised to see the kitchen empty save for Cal and Jayne, who were canoodling in a very familiar way in front of the sink. Jayne saw me and pulled away from the smooch. She cleared her throat and Cal turned toward me. His hair, normally fit for military inspection, was unwashed and tousled, still bearing the imprint of a pillow. He nodded at me and ran a hand through his coif.

"Morning, Miss Sadie," he said. "Sleep okay?"

"Why, yes, Cal, I did," I said, fighting the corners of my mouth from upturning. "I slept just fine, but I'll bet not as well as you." I raised my eyebrows and he blushed furiously.

Jayne put one hand over her mouth to hide her smile. Cal worked his mouth over to one side and bit his lower lip. Appearing to be at a total loss as to how to regain the safe, macho distance he'd worked so hard to build between us, he turned in his stocking feet and headed out the door. "I'll be in the shower."

I walked to the cupboard to retrieve a cup for coffee. "Is that a suggestion that you join him?" I asked Jayne, who *tsk*ed at me.

"Sadie," she said in her best scolding tone. By the nature of her job, she got much more scolding practice than I and would have been quite effective at it were it not for the goofy grin that accompanied her words. "Don't harass the poor man."

"Me?" I said incredulously. "I can't help it if I find just a teeny-weeny bit of joy in watching the man who had to hoist my rear into his pickup during our first meeting squirm a little."

Jayne handed me a plate heaped with food and pointed to the syrup on the table. "There's juice, too, when you're ready."

After a few bites of pancakes, I looked up to see Jayne staring at me. She sat down carefully in the chair across from me and, after a scan of the room for any wayward CIA operatives, whispered, "He said yes!" All propriety out the window, she clapped her hands together in one hard smack. "I'll start packing today."

And with that, Jayne proceeded to make the next ten days interminable. A host of problems arose. First was the List Problem. In a matter of hours, Jayne had bathed the rooms of her house with Post-it Notes declaring said room's importance in the daily life of the family. She didn't need to access the attic, thanks be to God, but the little fluorescent squares assaulted nearly every other corner of the house.

On the linen closet:
1. Towels for baths (Drew: red, Joel: blue, Emmy: pink)
2. Extra towels for Mac (dark green)
3. Emergency medical kit (Note: Band-Aids in downstairs med. chest.)

On the boys' bedroom door:
Bedtime ritual:
1. PJs (bottom drawer) and Pull-Ups (closet)
2. Brush teeth (Drew: Lightning McQueen toothbrush, blue. Joel: Tigger toothbrush, orange.)
3. Read two stories (they'll push for more)
4. Sing "Jesus Loves Me" twice
5. Pray
6. Humidifier to setting 2, lights out, door closed

On the back of Emmy's high chair:
Foods NOT allowed for baby:
1. PEANUT BUTTER
2. EGGS
3. POPCORN
4. NUTS
5. JAM WITH SEEDS
6. SODA, CANDY, EXCESSIVE SUGAR

This same list was posted on the refrigerator for backup.

By Wednesday, these things littered the kitchen,

bedrooms, and bathrooms. I couldn't believe that Cal would actually peruse them instead of just opening the closet door or the Tupperware drawer to see what was inside, but the note-taking seemed to make Jayne feel better so the rest of us played along.

Then came the Phone Problem. The calls began before I finished my pancakes Saturday, lasted until we had to discontinue the use of all electronic devices on the plane, and involved copious amounts of screaming. Here's an example:

(Phone rings. Jayne runs to answer it.)

"Hello? … Hiiiieeeee! I know, can you believe it? I'm going to the Big Apple! (Screaming) … Thursday to Sunday … Mac and Cal. I'm leaving lots of instructions … (Speaking away from the phone) Sadie, Lisa says you are the greatest!"

I nod and agree, then take my coffee cup with me as I leave the room.

(Jayne continues) "I don't know. I'm thinking Regis and Kelly for sure and maybe the Today show one morning. (Quietly) I'm hoping to run into John Travolta or Tom Cruise—maybe Sadie can introduce me! I definitely want to go to a Broadway musical, nothing too racy …"

I tried escaping to my room with dubious success. Inevitably, Jayne would rap quickly at the door—even that mundane action cheery and optimistic.

"Yes?" I'd call.

Jayne would open the door and ask her question, hand cupped over the mouthpiece of the phone. "Sadie, so sorry to bother you, but is Manhattan really an island?"

Or, "Is it true that most New Yorkers don't do their own laundry?"

Or, "Should I take pepper spray?"

At my replies to these questions, some more patient than others, Jayne would immediately relay the information to Jenni or Natalie or whomever shared the phone line at that moment, accompanied by dreamy sighs, squeals, or hushed and worried tones, as was appropriate.

In addition to the Post-its and the incessant phone calls, the final and most taxing problem was Jayne's conversation loop. From the Saturday morning of Cal's yes until we left for the airport a week and a half later, Jayne was stuck on a track and could not, no matter how I tried, be deterred from her musings on the following:

1. The survival of her children.
2. What New Yorkers wore compared with the fine people of Maplewood.
3. Times Square, Ground Zero, and Planet Hollywood, not always in that order.
4. The subway.

I did my best to warn her that a few days was not much in the city that never sleeps. (She loved that—"the city that never sleeps"—and began dropping it into conversation as often as she could.) Under normal conditions, visiting every tourist destination from the Statue of Liberty to the Guggenheim in a weekend was insane if not physically impossible. Plus, I told Jayne, as I was not known for my sightseeing enthusiasm and would need to be in rehearsals much of Saturday, our fanny-pack time was to be limited. Jayne would nod slowly, appearing to think about the weight of these considerations. And then she'd start in on what shoes to bring (we'd walk a lot—probably Nikes, right?), whether she should freeze one lasagna or two, and if she should budget for subway rides or cabs.

The entire planning phase drained me of any enthusiasm I'd held in those brief moments after the attic miniconcert. And our feet were still firmly rooted on the frozen ground of Iowa.

15

Multiculturalism

Wednesday night finally arrived, the night before Jayne and I were scheduled to take Heartland Air 1098 from Maplewood to New York, with a layover in O'Hare. I was up in the attic, filling one of my large Louis Vuittons. After Jayne left Sunday to go back home, I'd remain for the rest of spring break week, luxuriating in the comforts of congestion, good food, and imported chocolate. I hummed to myself as I packed, imagining morning walks through the Park, flaky croissants as a reward for my physical exertion, and rehearsals with people who knew good coffee. It was nearly ten o'clock and the rest of the house was quiet with sleep. Youngest to oldest, the Hartleys had retired early that evening, the kids worn out at the end of the day, Cal exhausted from a debacle involving an infertile boar, and Jayne weary from all her Post-its, plans, and packing.

As I folded my pink cashmere turtleneck and laid it carefully on one side of the suitcase, I felt someone watching me. I looked up and saw a man in a ball cap standing in the shadows of the staircase, his eyes peeking over where the floor met the railing. In the split second before I let out a glass-shattering scream, Mac was up the rest of the stairs and pulling me to him.

"Just hush a minute," he said. "It's only me. You want to wake up the whole house?" His eyes sparkled, even in the dark room.

I pulled away and stood with hands on my hips. "What, exactly, do you think you're doing, spying on me in my room? How did you get in here?"

He rolled his eyes. "People around here don't have six locks on their doors because we *trust* each other. And even if Cal did lock his door, don't you think his own brother would get an extra key?" He flopped down on the chair by the window and crossed one long leg over the other. He wore dark blue jeans and polished boots. Spring had made a tip-toed entrance that afternoon. Mac wore a long-sleeved dark green shirt but no coat.

"Please," I said, the sarcasm dripping, "do make yourself at home, Mr. Hartley. Can I get you anything? Tea? Coffee? Piece of pie?" I stood glaring at him, arms crossed over my worn Eastman sweatshirt.

Mac chuckled. "Let me assure you, Miss Sadie Maddox, if I were looking for a good piece of pie, you would not be my first stop."

"Well," I said huffily, "how about you tell me why you *are* here, if it isn't for my hospitality."

He stood and put his hands in his pockets. "Let's go." He walked to the top of the stairs.

"Excuse me?"

"Time for you to get out of this house."

I shook my head, utterly confused. "I'm perfectly happy in this house. I'm packing to go to New York tomorrow."

Mac nodded quickly. "That's my point. How long have you been in Maplewood? Two months?"

I nodded. "About that."

Mac walked over to me and took my hand, pulling me toward the stairs. "Exactly. Two months and all you've done is sing, eat, sleep, and aggravate your chauffeur service. I'm not letting you go back to your snooty New York friends and tell them there's nothing to do around here or that we're just a bunch of hicks."

"But I'm not ready to go out." I looked down at my ensemble: sweatshirt, jeans that were definitely past their prime, sporty shoes I'd gotten off a rack in Chinatown. In short, I was perfectly dressed to wash dishes.

Mac sized me up, taking his own sweet time and letting a smile creep across his face. "You look perfect. This isn't some hoity-toity Manhattan night club." He started down the stairs, his hand still holding mine. "Now," he said, turning to face me. His eyes, remarkable at this short distance, were level with mine. I took a sharp breath. "You think we can get out of here without waking the troops? I don't feel the need to include my little brother and his sweet wife in my nighttime wanderings."

I nodded, my heart racing despite itself, and followed him in silence, straight out the door and toward an adventure.

♪

The Roadhouse sat at the bottom of a hill on the edge of a neighboring town named Clayton. Mac pulled up to the rambling building sided with brown shingles and trimmed in a horrible orange-red. A blinking neon sign crowned the roof and featured a cowboy on a rearing bull.

Mac turned his truck into an empty space in the gravel parking lot and cut the engine. He turned to me, his face blinking red and blue in time to the sign. "Ready for some music education?"

I sighed. "Country dancing."

He grinned, lips pushed out in a gesture of cocky victory.

"I'd hoped you were whisking me away to a little known hole-in-the-wall French restaurant, owned and run by a family known only to the discerning few and cherished for their world-class *coq au vin*."

Mac let a puff of air escape his mouth in a gesture of disbelief or impatience, I couldn't tell which. "You sure seem to have an active inner life, as Oprah would say."

I raised my eyebrows. "You watch Oprah."

"Nah," he said, hand on the door handle. "But sounding like I do impresses the ladies." He winked and unfolded out of the cab.

I waited for him as he strode in front of the truck toward my door. When he opened it, I stood on the running board, happy to have a small moment where I could tower over him. I pointed my finger at his nose. "I'll participate in your uncouth form of dancing to music that demeans women and glorifies alcohol, cowboys, and trucks."

Mac cocked his head and smiled. "Sounds perfect."

"But." I wagged my finger in his face. "I forbid you to make fun of my footwork, get me intoxicated, or otherwise humiliate me." I lifted my chin and looked down on him. "And I might have to be taken somewhere else to use the restroom if the one here is as revolting as I suspect it to be."

Mac lifted me up and set me down gently on the ground. He kept his arms around me, letting the warmth from his hands linger on my sweatshirt. He looked into my eyes, which were wide and much like a deer's in that moment.

"What's Eastman?" he asked softly, nodding at the lettering on my sweatshirt.

"A music school. Very prestigious," I said quietly, lightheaded at being this close to him.

"Never heard of it," he said, pulling away and turning me toward the neon. "Let's dance," he said, and slapped me on the rear. Hard.

I walked slightly behind him, not sure whether I'd just been rebuffed or seduced. My rump hurt, in either case, and I hobbled along behind him, wincing at the sting.

Mac held the door for me. I stepped past him and into another realm of neon, this time a pantheon to cheap beer draped in signage above the bar. Mac stood next to me and hollered a greeting to the bartender, a hefty woman in a denim shirt with *Roadhouse* embroidered on the pocket. I expected it to blink if I stared long enough.

"Hey, Mac," she said, ambling toward us. "How're things?"

"Good, good," Mac said, taking off his cap and laying it on the bar. "How about yourself, Danelle?"

"Fine," Danelle said. She wiped out a glass with a white towel, sizing me up in a most unhurried fashion.

I patted my hair, surprised anew that I'd been coerced out of my home looking this disheveled. Then again, Danelle in her denim wasn't exactly mugging for Fashion Week either.

She smacked her gum and placed the shiny clean glass on a shelf below the bar. "What can I get you two?"

"I'll have a Bud." He turned to me.

I didn't think it productive to ask about the Roadhouse's wine cellar. "Yes. Right. I'll have cranberry juice, very little ice."

Danelle raised one eyebrow, still chomping on her gum, but obediently turned to retrieve our drinks. I took stock of our company. Two older men sat at the end of the bar, gray-haired, in farmer caps, and watching us in silence. At a small table near the dance floor sat a couple, the woman in her twenties with a profusion of red curls and the man, in his fifties or so, looking like a smug cat as she leaned over the table and whispered in his ear. I felt a strong urge to inform the woman that those ears likely grew long, bristly hairs that she would be called upon to pluck, should she stick around. But I was pulled back by Danelle's husky voice.

"Here you go," she said, sliding a full tumbler of juice toward me.

Mac cleared his throat before anybody got too nosy. "We're here to dance, even if nobody else is." He slapped a five down on the bar. "Turn up the music when you get a chance, will you?" He smiled at Danelle and picked up his beer.

I followed him to a table opposite the mature man and his trophy. I nodded over to them. "I'm assuming she's not his niece."

Mac took a swig of his beer and watched them over the lip of the glass. His eyes were very serious, taking in the scene as if it were an early Botticelli. "He's a fool," he said finally, cupping one hand around his glass.

My heart swelled with joy at having heard such words from an attractive man in my age group. There was hope! All was not lost in the world!

"If I was gonna get a young one like that, I'd at least make sure she was good-looking."

"You are an infuriating man."

He burrowed his hand into the small snack bowl between us and popped a handful of the orange-hued mix into his mouth. Even in the dismal lighting in the Roadhouse, I could see his eyes twinkling with mirth.

"And you are likely eating something prepared in 1998 in the bowels of a New Jersey snack mix plant." I shook my head, not even trying to fend off the blanket of despair that was beginning to cloak me. *How has it come to this?* I chastised myself. So I hadn't been on a date in awhile. Did that mean I had to settle for fossilized peanuts with a man who drank Budweiser?

Mac threw back his head, pushed his chair back until he balanced on only two legs, and laughed with such gusto it took him a moment to compose himself. I sat with my arms crossed, watching the redhead trace circles on the palm of pimp daddy's hand.

"Now, now," Mac said, letting his chair regain its rightful pose and leaning over the table to me. He waited until I looked him in the eye. "You and I both know that man is looking to embarrass himself."

"He is?" I said, fiddling with the cocktail napkin under my cranberry juice.

"Yes, he is." He reached over and detracted my busy fingers from the napkin. He ran one finger slowly along each of mine. *If only he'd waited one more week*, I thought, entranced. Then I would have had a decent manicure.

"Not only that," he said, "but it is the humble opinion of this man that a woman becomes more beautiful with age, so that poor chap is missing the boat."

I looked at him skeptically, waiting for the shoe to drop. "But?" I said and pulled my hand away. I narrowed my eyes. "She's probably a good romp in the meantime?"

"Sadie Maddox!" Mac said, his eyes bulging in feigned offense. "Such language coming from a world famous opera star! You charm your public with that mouth?"

As much as I would have liked to deny him the pleasure, I could not contain my laughter.

He pushed away from the table. "Enough chitchat, sweetheart. All this verbalizing of feelings is wearing me out." He offered me his hand to help me up. "Time for your first lesson in the two-step."

We hit the floor during a song that praised in no uncertain terms the full-figured woman. I found this to be exceptionally heartening and made myself teachable under the capable tutelage of Mac. Having no other experience with which to compare him and as we were the only couple on the floor, I hated to be too impressed, but he did appear to be a very good dancer. As with other forms of dance accepted by more civilized people, the man's role in the dance was crucial. A good lead could make or break every single eight-count. But I was in good hands, literally. Mac spun me, whirled me, dipped me, twirled me, and I laughed like a schoolgirl for the first time in a long time.

"You have very good rhythm," he yelled over the music.

"Thank you," I yelled back. "Could you call the Met and put in a good word?"

He chuckled, which I took to mean he'd at least heard of the Met. After two more wild songs, one about going fishing and ditching the wife to do it and the other about getting revenge on a boyfriend by torching his house, we slowed down and danced to a ballad.

A woman sang in a lush alto about a man who loved her despite her cheating heart. We moved slowly back and forth, Mac's arms around me and our feet barely shifting on the floor. I felt a happy exhaustion settling in and allowed myself the deliciousness of resting my head on his chest. My hair, I assumed, hung in dreadful, limp strands anyway by that point, not only because of my unexpected foray to the honky-tonk but also because I hadn't let it be touched by any of the "stylists" in Maplewood. Going to my salon in New York and letting Jack get his hands on the disaster was one of the first items on the next week's agenda.

Unable to stifle it, I yawned with a flourish into Mac's chest. He spoke into my ear in order to be heard above the music. "Tired?"

I nodded.

We finished the song and he led me off the floor and out the door, waving to Danelle as we left. The sudden quiet of the night outside magnified the sound of our footsteps on the gravel. Mac let me into the truck and jogged around to his side. I shivered in my sweatshirt.

"Warmer days now but our nights will be cool for awhile yet." Mac said, cranking the heat as we pulled onto the highway.

"I had fun," I said, smiling at myself for the truth of those words.

"Good." He sounded pleased. "That was the goal."

We sat in silence the rest of the ride home, much like we did during our morning and evening commutes. I felt something had changed between us, come alive almost, and I wondered if I was the only one who'd noticed.

Mac cut the lights on his truck before turning down the long driveway toward Cal and Jayne's.

"Now," he said as we slowed to a stop near the front sidewalk. "You tell those big city friends of yours we know how to have good time in the middle of nowhere, too. Next time," he said as he opened his door, "I'll take you to work with me. Show you how to perform an autopsy on a horse."

"Why, I ask you, did you have to ruin this moment?"

I shuddered to think of that field trip.

We crept toward the house, hand in hand, not unlike two wily teenagers out past curfew. Mac turned the front doorknob with the finesse of a burglar and moved aside. I made no noise stepping over the threshold; Mac raised his eyebrows and nodded, impressed with my work. I waved and smiled then moved to close the door but Mac reached for me and pulled me to him. He leaned down and kissed me softly. I closed my eyes, inhaling sharply the scent of him. He pulled away. I took a breath to speak but he put a finger over his lips to shush me. In general, I do not appreciate being shushed, but considering the moment, I obliged.

I stepped back and he closed the door, leaving me to tiptoe in silent wonder up to my room.

16

The Big Apple

"Oh. My. Good. Gracious." Jayne stood in capri pants, tennis shoes, and fanny pack and looked up. Her mouth formed an O, the back of her head tilted so her pale hair vibrated in a small, suspended arc. "I can't believe I'm here." She wiped away a tear at the corner of her eye.

I rolled my eyes, certain that Jayne wouldn't notice and that I wouldn't have cared if she had. These kinds of exclamations had traveled with us to the Statue of Liberty and the viewing deck of the Empire State Building and it was only two in the afternoon. There was only so much I could do before unveiling the superhuman effort it was taking not to kill myself. For all my bravado about avoiding tourist traps, I'd succumbed to guilt and had agreed to shuttle my guest around to some of New York's most popular attractions. I'd put my foot down at seeing *Mary Poppins*, the only Broadway show with tickets available. But I'd been unable to deny Jayne the pleasure of a double-decker bus and now, Forty-second Street.

"Times Square in New York City," Jayne said, shaking her head. "I watch every year when the ball drops but I had no idea how impressive it would be in person."

I wouldn't have used that particular adjective, I thought as I gathered in our surroundings. Overrun by people with cameras, yes. Chock-full of overpriced, unimaginative food, yes. The object of many a native New Yorker's disdain, absolutely. But impressive? I sighed again and started walking. Jayne followed closely behind, taking two steps for every one of mine.

"Where are we going?" she asked excitedly. People jostled us on every side and I felt Jayne's hand find my elbow.

"Late lunch with Richard. Are you hungry?"

"Famished," she said. I glanced at her face. It would not be overly dramatic to say she glowed. The woman had been smiling almost without fail since we stepped onto the puddle jumper in Maplewood. I had definitely underestimated how ready Jayne had been to get out of dodge. Certain the plane ride (her first) would present various challenges, I'd tucked into my handbag a packet of Dramamine, chewing gum for help with ascent and descent, and had given the gate attendant a heads-up before boarding that we had with us a first-time flyer who might become hysterical.

Not a peep.

Jayne had remained calm and unperturbed, happy to peruse her *Today's Christian Woman* through a teeth-grinding ascent, in turbulence over Lake Michigan, and during a particularly trying odor incident in the final leg that had compelled me to use my air purifier. In fact, she had been the one to comfort me when I'd gone green from the smell.

"We're almost to La Guardia," she'd said like a native, patting my hand and taking a sip of ginger ale.

She'd been thoroughly appreciative of my apartment, commenting cheerily on the furnishings, which she assured me were very "fancy," and she'd been keeping the living room, where she slept, impeccably clean. She'd even had the guts to leave the building early the first morning and with directions from Tom the doorman, had walked a block to my grocer to pick up essentials for breakfast. *Just like on the farm,* I thought, Jayne took care of my culinary needs without being asked.

Lunch, though, had the potential to put a deep wrinkle in her Pollyanna outlook.

"Jayne," I said, turning a corner at a clip. "Are you familiar with Japanese food?"

"Nooo," she said slowly and not without a dollop of concern.

"I've made plans to meet Richard at a Japanese noodle place a few blocks from here. Are you up for it?"

"*Um,* yes."

"Because Times Square has plenty of places to eat, if you'd prefer something safer." *And if you'd like to get suckered into a twenty-five-dollar plate of burger and fries like all these other saps,* I thought as we passed a flock of them wearing matching Hard Rock Café T-shirts.

We walked a few paces before she answered. "I'd like to go with you, if that's all right." She watched my face as we walked. "But I'll need help ordering. I don't speak Japanese."

I turned to her and laughed. I draped my arm around her tiny shoulders and squeezed her to me as we walked. "Jayne Hartley, you are impossibly perfect."

She grinned and scurried along to keep up with my stride.

We reached the restaurant and my mouth began to water before I even opened the door. Although Richard and I had been here countless times, neither of us was sure of the restaurant's name. We referred to it simply as the Unbelievable Noodle Place Off Times Square. The place was unbelievable for two reasons. First, the décor. Perhaps as a nod to its proximity to Times Square, the owners had ramped up the corny factor to new heights. Water features filled the place, several of them spilling into mini koi ponds where the "koi" were actually overfed goldfish. Fake greenery spilled from every crevice. A silver wallpaper border topped the pale peach walls. The crowning glory, a self-playing pink upright piano, stood in the middle of the restaurant and played easy-listening classics like the themes from *Chariots of Fire* and *Ice Castles*.

Quixotic ambience notwithstanding, the food at the Unbelievable Noodle Place Off Times Square had transformative powers and was unfathomably inexpensive. This was the second reason for its treasured place in our collective memory. A girl could immerse herself in a vat of steaming ramen and forget very easily that goldfish were swimming only inches away from her feet and that "Mandy" was not, in fact, her favorite song. All this for under ten dollars.

"Sadie!" Richard broadsided me and immersed me in a hug. He smelled of expensive pipe tobacco and cologne.

I pulled away to see his face. We kissed both cheeks and I laughed at the pleasure of seeing him. "So, so good to see you," I said. "You look fantastic."

"I do, don't I?" he said, stepping away so I could get the full view. He turned to my guest. "Jayne. You are lovely." He leaned over to kiss her flushed cheek and her eyes widened at me over his shoulder.

"Jayne Hartley," I said, "meet my dear friend and former husband, Richard LaSalle."

"It's very nice to meet you." Jayne smiled and blushed, blushed and smiled, while Richard soaked up every bit of it like the last drops of French onion soup at the bottom of a bowl. "In person, that is," Jayne added shyly.

"Oh, yes, yes," Richard said, remembering. "We spoke on the phone that one morning. I believe you were on the way to church. Our table's ready," he said, ushering us to a four-top by the windows. "Church, right. Did Sadie tell you about how it was the *church* that compelled her to spend the semester in Iowa?"

I shot him a look, and he grinned like the Cheshire cat as he pulled out Jayne's chair. I seated myself.

"No, she didn't," Jayne said. She looked at me, confused. "You mean like a missions trip?"

Richard cackled and said through his laughter, "Yes, something like that."

I cleared my throat. "Jayne, it is imperative that you remember, in all your dealings with Richard, that he is not known for his truthfulness. Nor his discretion," I added, narrowing my eyes across the table.

"Now, now," Richard said, reaching for my hand. "You know you love me. Have you missed me horribly or am I the only one who's been miserable?"

Jayne watched us with big eyes. A fleeting image of Mac and his quiet, deep laughter passed through my mind. I patted Richard's hand and pulled mine out of his grasp.

"Of course I've missed you," I said, smiling and studying his face. "You look well. How are things?"

As always, diverting the focus of the conversation to Richard himself worked beautifully in distracting from the issue at hand. He launched into a dramatic telling of the fiasco of the week, an errant stage manager at Juilliard who had placed the wrong score on Richard's stand for one of the pieces he'd conducted at a weekend concert. Jayne listened with polite attention, though I suspected she was bored out of her mind. The food presented challenge enough for her once our dishes began to arrive. She huddled over her bowl of noodles, looking about half her age as she tried to decipher all the ingredients in the broth. I flagged down a waiter and asked for Western flatware after she'd struggled valiantly with her chopsticks and soupspoon for a good five minutes.

"So, Jayne." Richard said at the end of the meal. He pushed his empty bowl toward the center of the table and wiped the edges of his mouth with a rose-colored cloth napkin. "Is this your first time to New York?"

She nodded. "I love it," she said, embarrassed at once by her exaggerated enthusiasm. "Sorry. I'm sure I sound like a country bumpkin, but I do love it. I love the different kinds of people, the energy, the *bigness* of everything. It's *so* much better than Branson."

Richard looked confused.

"Missouri," I said. "*Hee Haw* meets Las Vegas, if you will."

"Ah," he said, nodding. Bemusement spilled out of his eyes. "So they have shows in Branson?"

"Oh, yes," Jayne said. "Lots of them. It's mostly country and bluegrass, but they have some gospel, too."

"Well, there you go," Richard said with a gesture of finality. "I'm sure they're looking for singers, wouldn't you think? Sadie? Are you available?" He chided me with a boyish grin.

"Sure," I said. I took a big gulp of iced tea, no lemon. "Why not? I'll just travel from loser town to loser town, racking up professional derision and humiliation."

Richard stopped swirling his glass of dessert wine. His eyebrows arched and he looked at Jayne's face. I swallowed and turned to her. "Jayne," I said, guilt oozing out of even that one solitary word. "I didn't mean—"

"Don't worry about it," she said brightly. "You're right."

"No, I'm not," I said, fumbling. "Maplewood is a wonderful place for … casseroles. And farm machinery. And soybeans." I looked at Richard, who appeared to be enjoying watching me squirm. "Raising children!" I said triumphantly. "It's a great place to raise kids, right?"

"Absolutely," she said, flashing me a forced smile. She resumed poking at a cold lump of bok choy.

"It's just that I hadn't planned on being in Iowa at this point in my career," I concluded feebly.

"Speaking of your career," Richard said, "Judith told me she might be able to open up an appointment for you while you're in the city." He leaned forward in his chair with an air of conspiracy. "She told me she has some ideas for your return to New York in the summer."

"Really?" I said, feeling my heart pound in my chest. "Like …?"

He shrugged, reveling in his superior position of One Who Knew Dirt. "Without going into specifics, I believe it has to do with a new recording contract, some sort of compilation with four other hot-to-trot classical singers, kind of a 'Best of Puccini' with hints of 'American Idol' thrown in for good measure. Solo numbers *and* ensemble pieces. And then," he paused dramatically, "a ten-city domestic tour followed by a spring tour in Europe. They're billing it '*Pasione*.'"

"What?" I jumped in my seat, high enough to make the water in our glasses slosh over the rims. "And she wants *me?* Why?"

Richard shook his head. "Sadie, has Iowa sucked all the confidence out of you?" He looked at Jayne. "No offense."

"I can't believe it." I stared at the wall beyond Richard, lost in thought. "Avi hasn't said a word."

"What, and distract him from booking a bigger check with the same tour?" Richard sighed. "Darling, I hate to be the one to break it to you, but Avi's been doing a masterful job agenting for Reneé, Kiri, and Cecilia, all of whom, like yourself, remember fondly the era of disco." He gathered both my hands in his. "The plateau in your career is not now, nor has it ever been, an age issue. It's an *agent* issue."

An agent issue, I thought as I signed the check. *Not an age issue*, I thought as we meandered a few blocks together before taking separate cabs, Jayne and I back up to my apartment and Richard to a rehearsal in midtown. The precarious hope Richard offered was enough to make me feel dizzy.

"Jayne, again, I'm sorry for my comment about Maplewood." Her uncharacteristic silence was unnerving.

"Don't be," she said, watching a man fly past us on a bike. "You've got a lot on your mind right now."

I looked out my window as the streets of Manhattan paraded by, mulling over the images of a renewed career that pushed Jayne and Maplewood quietly to the periphery. *Too soon to hope, too soon to hope*, I told myself and could feel every wishful thought soar in blissful ignorance.

17

Spring Awakening

"*Mmmm. Mmmm. Mmmph.*" I could hear Jayne's moaning through the thin walls of the day spa. I looked up through my avocado and cucumber mask and saw Simone's eyes widen. "It's her first facial," I said, closing my eyes and sighing. "First time to New York, first encounter with a homeless person, first cab ride. It's been a weekend of firsts."

"Ah," Simone said. She massaged my temples and I did *not* moan, though I wanted to. "We get that reaction a lot, actually. Just not usually with such volume."

For being such a little slip of a thing, Jayne had thrown herself into her New York adventure like a force three times her size. Other than the quiet cab ride the

day before, she'd had an effusive, childlike reaction
to every part of her trip. The coffee at Tasia's felt like
fireworks in her mouth, she'd said, and had taken
long, luxuriant sips. The spring green of Central Park
was the most vibrant she'd ever seen (clearly under the
NYC influence by this point as the woman was from
Iowa). The pasta at La Piazza had "changed her life."
I dared not let myself hope that was true, as returning
to goulash was going to be a challenge. But the delight
that she had in the mundane soon spread to her hostess
as well. We'd decided on a trip to the spa as one final
celebration before my rehearsal that evening and her
flight out the following morning.

When we met up in the spa's waiting area, I laughed
out loud.

"That was incredible." Her face shone with
moisturizer and her eyelids were still relaxed into slits. "I
can't believe I'm thirty years old and I've never done that
before. Why didn't you tell me?" She sent me a sleepy,
betrayed look.

I opened the door and held it for her. "It never came
up." I breathed in a decadent dose of spring air laced with
only trace amounts of exhaust and sewage. It was a good
day for oxygen in New York. "But where would a girl go,
anyway, to get a facial in Maplewood?"

She shook her head mournfully. "Rhonda does hair
and nails but she doesn't do facials. I suppose I could call
over to Landsmere, see if their salon does them."

Landsmere, a hovel of two hundred, sat farther down
the highway than Mac's Roadhouse hangout. To be honest,
I didn't hold high hopes for a decent spa treatment to be
had one mile before the outskirts of Chicago, which were

a good four hours from Maplewood. But why dampen the perfection of a post-massage moment?

"Let's stop for gelato on the way home, shall we?"

Jayne brightened. This would be the third of our visits to a gelateria close to my apartment. It would save me more than a few calories when Jayne's plane took off on Sunday, though I was sure my endorphins would suffer as well.

"Mac called," Jayne said when we'd settled at a table with our dessert. She licked at a spoonful of *frutti di bosco*, leaving a deep pink stain on her lips.

"Did he?" I watched Jayne's face, searching for any knowledge of our late-night adventure the evening before we'd flown to New York.

She nodded. "Said everybody's doing fine. In fact," she said, gathering a small mountain of gelato onto her spoon, "I think those kids are going to lobby for me to leave more often. They've had pizza every night, waffles and ice cream for breakfast, and got to watch four movies in two days." She shook her head. "Those men are useless."

"So true," I said, knowing full well the children would have been picked up by Children and Family Services had I been left in charge. "Did he say anything else?" I took a big bite of my *limone*.

"Let's see." She swirled her spoon around in thought. "Oh, yes, actually. He said to give you a message. It was really weird …" She scrunched her nose, searching for the words. "I think he said to tell you some woman named Danelle would like to talk to you about giving lessons."

I suppressed a smile by filling my mouth with gelato.

Jayne shrugged. "Singing lessons, I guess, though I don't know why she'd contact Mac about something like that."

"How odd," I said, feeling a sharp pang in my chest as I realized I missed him. *Smart aleck,* I thought, and knew he'd smiled into the phone when he'd relayed his message. Lessons, indeed.

"I'm really looking forward to sitting in on your rehearsal tonight." Jayne folded her paper napkin into a neat square and tucked it into her empty dish. "Are you sure it's all right?"

"Of course," I said, sitting up straighter and smiling at her pixie face. "When one is the soloist, one can do whatever one wants."

♪

That promise proved to be more difficult to keep than I'd anticipated. Our rehearsal was not slated to be open to the public. Maurice, the conductor, and Julian, the artistic director at St. Bart's, made a show of intense, whispered debate, rife with dramatic hand gestures and heated remarks. Finally, Julian relented and allowed Jayne to sit in the empty theater, after I promised she was merely a humble midwestern housewife unable to make the concert Thursday and not, in fact, a spy from Lincoln Center, lying in wait to plot his professional demise and financial failure. I rolled my eyes at Jayne, awash in fresh disbelief at the theatrics embedded in my career. Honestly, at times I couldn't imagine how an even-keeled person like me survived in such an environment.

I sat off to the side of the stage while the orchestra warmed up. My rehearsal water was tepid, but I'd already had the stage manager change it twice. If the word *lukewarm* doesn't register after two times, was there really hope for the third? After several minutes, Maurice tapped his baton on the edge of his music stand. "People," he said, "we'll start with the Handel, then the Mozart, and then the orchestral pieces. But first," he said, turning to me with a flourish, "let us welcome the divine Sadie Maddox."

I waved to the strings, the winds, the brass. Orchestral applause was a rare bird, all of it muted because it's made with the players' feet. Not even Sadie Maddox could make a violinist lay down her weapon and clap like a normal person. Maurice reached for my hand and kissed it. Even with the extra foot of height offered by the conductor's podium, I towered over the little man. He dropped my hand abruptly and whacked his baton on the stand again.

"All right," he said. "'He Shall Feed His Flock.'"

Maurice and Julian had called about the program choices six months earlier. They'd billed the concert "Sacred and Sublime," and had decided on a full program of sacred works. The two men had been particularly giddy about performing the Handel in March. They'd selected two arias from *Messiah*, the oratorio famous for its "Hallelujah" chorus. Julian insisted they were renegades to program selections from the piece any time other than November and December, and Maurice had agreed to their slap in the face of the traditional music establishment, assuming there was one of those in New York. This was the city that showcased nude interpretive dance, live jazz inside a giant aquarium, and accordion improv for octogenarians, and that was within the space of one weekend. I questioned the depth of their rebellion but was content to be hired.

The melody of the first aria lifted out of the violins. "He shall feed His flock like a shepherd," I began, filling the space between me and Jayne, who sat in the center of the balcony. I could see her smiling and watching my face. "And He shall gather the lambs with His arm, and carry them in His bosom, and gently lead those that are with young."

I needed to rehearse the transition again but Maurice continued undeterred to the modulation. "Come unto him," I sang, "ye that are heavy laden and He will give you rest." Jayne nodded slightly in time to the music, and I wondered if she were dreading her own return to the life of a heavy-laden farm wife. *Never,* I thought, *could I do what she does.* Better to resign myself to anonymity for the rest of my life than to live with three small children in the middle of a field. I could hear my tone becoming disengaged and unnecessarily dark as I considered it, so I regained my focus and finished the piece.

After chipping away at some less-than-inspired phrasing on the part of the orchestra, Maurice seemed satisfied for the moment and launched us into the more triumphant "I Know That My Redeemer Liveth." Though the piece was written for a high soprano, my upper range was more expansive than the average mezzo and, when in good voice, was able to soar on the high G-sharps. I would have much preferred to "soar" on high Gs and had said as much to Maurice and Julian. However, they'd been unwilling to perform the piece in anything but its original key and stuck with E major, a key that had never been my best.

My start was rocky. All the way through the first phrases of "I know that my Redeemer liveth, and that He shall stand at the latter day upon the earth," my voice sounded sluggish. I couldn't seem to move air through to the ends of phrases. Maurice was starting to send me snooty glances from his podium. I was ruminating on his bad shoes and on Julian's rigidity with key changes when my eyes lit on Jayne's face. Tears streamed down her cheeks. She made no effort to wipe them away, simply sat with hands clasped in her lap, eyes trained on me and washed in the music.

I could feel my heart begin to race. Turning my eyes away from Jayne, I couldn't help but feel nervous. The last time someone had experienced such a physical reaction to my singing, I'd packed up and moved to a town that hadn't heard of Kalamata olives. *Things are finally looking up in my career,* I found myself praying. *Please don't mess with me now.*

We finished the piece, and Maurice told me pointedly that we had a few days before the dress rehearsal and that perhaps I'd acclimate to Eastern Standard Time by then. I smiled, trying my best not to feel like a schoolgirl given detention, and bid him and the orchestra farewell until Wednesday.

When Jayne met me in the lobby, she threw her arms around me and stayed there until there was no semblance of social propriety left. I gently pulled away. She brushed a tear from her cheek.

"I know too," she said, her eyes intensely blue after crying.

"You do?" I said. *What, exactly, does she know?* I thought. About the John the Baptist moment? About my late-night two-stepping with Mac?

She nodded. "I *do* know my Redeemer liveth." Her eyes filled with new tears. She took a deep breath and I became concerned she was readying herself to sing the piece herself.

"Jayne," I said, putting a hand on her arm. *Keep her calm,* I thought. If Maurice wasn't thrilled about her sitting in on the rehearsal, when he heard her chirping Handel from the lobby, he might use his baton as an impaling device.

Jayne followed me gamely as I led her through the narthex and down a small flight of stairs. We pushed open a set of heavy doors and were greeted with blinding March sunshine. I squinted into my Chanel purse, searching for my sunglasses case.

"Just look: the sun, the spring—all this rebirth practically begging me to stop and look." Jayne swept her hand across the courtyard that bordered one side of the building. "Easter is just around the corner, and you know what?" I didn't, but she rambled right along anyway. "Until I heard you singing today, I hadn't given it a bit of thought." She laughed ruefully. "The One who redeems me from a life of emptiness *lives* and I've been too busy to notice." She stepped onto the bottom rung of a railing that encircled a small birch tree. Soon buds would pepper the brittle branches but now they stood shivering in the cool breeze. "He is risen!" Jayne shouted, balancing her weight on the railing and throwing one small hand into the air.

Have mercy, I thought, looking around the courtyard and hoping no one from the orchestra was en route for a smoke break.

"I said, 'He is risen!'" Jayne nodded toward me.

"All right, all right," I muttered, crowded suddenly with musty memories of Easter Sunday and uncomfortable, starched dresses. I knew what to do to shut her up. "He is risen indeed!" I said, finishing with a dramatic sigh. I could practically hear my mother applauding from her vantage point in glory.

"Amen!" Jayne trilled. She jumped down from her perch, her face triumphant and glowing even more luminously than after the white tea mask and exfoliating massage. She pulled me into a fierce embrace. "Thank you, Sadie, for reminding me of what and Who is most important."

I patted her slowly on her back, feeling even in that gesture the surprising frailty of her frame. She clung to me and I felt tears sting my eyes. I blinked furiously, staring at a flock of wispy clouds that were parading like royalty across the baby blue sky. *Redeemed from a life of emptiness,* I thought, pushing back at the thought with what little reserve I had in that moment.

Jayne pulled away and tried with little success to hide her surprise at my red nose and smudged mascara. She pulled a tissue out of her purse and handed it to me without a word.

"Reminds me of Easter when I was a girl," I said feebly before blowing my nose, never a dainty sound no matter how one tries.

Jayne nodded and allowed a small smile. "I know just how you feel," she said. She looped her arm in mine and we started on a long walk, drinking in the light that follows winter.

18

Lonely Hearts

Jayne left for the airport the following morning with a poker face. I tried in vain to convince her to take a cab instead of the bus but she was feeling heady with enthusiasm for Gotham City, public transportation included, and could not be dissuaded.

"I'll be fine," she said, as if to a henpecking mother concerned about curfew violations. "I'm completely up on the M60 line."

"May I submit one final vote for a cab? It's so much easier and not that expensive."

Jayne's face betrayed no impatience, though we'd discussed this forty-five times. "Thirty dollars for a cab, but only two for the bus. The bus is far more interesting for people watching. And if I have any trouble, I can ask one of the transit people. Isn't it their job to help people like me?"

"Technically, yes," I said, though they could also eat you, depending on their mood. I sighed dramatically and put my hand on my apartment doorknob.

"Okay, then," she said, reaching over for a final, quick hug. She pulled out the handle of her rolling carry-on and hefted her purse over her shoulder. The woman must have had a vacuum sealer in that suitcase because it would have fit no more than one complete ensemble for me and maybe a toothbrush. But she'd looked clean and pressed, though not quite fashionable, all weekend living out of that thing. Resourceful people, those midwesterners.

"See you back in Maplewood," she said, and with a wave, she was gone.

I watched her until she disappeared in the elevator. With the door shut behind me, I stood looking at my empty apartment, feeling restless. The bus issue wasn't what bothered me. Jayne had done quite a bit of wandering during her few days in New York and I was reasonably sure that she'd make it to LaGuardia just fine. She did have a cell phone and my number in case she needed it. No, it wasn't public transportation that was so unsettling, though many in my city would disagree with that statement.

I plopped down on the couch, still in my soft Egyptian cotton pajamas and pink slippers. Clouds had moved in overnight and blanketed Manhattan in a chilly shroud. *It's loneliness,* I thought, and immediately hated myself for thinking the words. After two months of living in a house with constant action and then having Jayne stay with me for my first weekend home, I had become accustomed to people. I shuddered. *Shrug it off,* I said to myself, running a hand over my makeup-free face. *You're just readjusting to* normal *life,* functional *life, life away from small children and farm smells.*

I hopped up from the couch and scurried to the bathroom, hungry for the mental cleanse a hot shower promised. I made it a point to sing loudly enough to let my neighbors know I was home.

"Let's take it from the pickup to bar forty," Maurice said, tapping that infernal baton so loudly I could barely hear his directions. We were forty-five minutes into our dress rehearsal, and the second Handel piece, the one that inspired a spiritual epiphany for Jayne, was causing a decidedly different reaction in Maurice. The orchestra sounded sloppy and anemic concerning the straightforwardness of the parts. And I sounded, well, provincial. My ornamentation labored instead of spun. I felt like my vocal chords were swimming through a swamp, fully clothed and gasping for a deep breath.

By the time we'd run "Redeemer" three times, I was feeling incrementally better and Maurice seemed placated. After many years of singing, I'd become accustomed to having a temperamental instrument. Because singing required total physical engagement from a singer, vocal perfection could be elusive and fussy. A late evening, poor sleep, strange diet, even a low barometer reading could make one feel "off." The professional developed techniques and survival skills to shake off whatever ailed or work through it so that no one but the singer herself noticed. *You're doing fine,* I pep talked myself as I left the stage, water bottle and score in hand. *You're putting too much pressure on your reentry to the concert arena.* I nodded, absorbed in the need to convince, willing my head to believe its own soliloquy.

"Sadie."

I lifted my head from reverie. "Avi," I said, dropping my score on one of the velvet-upholstered seats on the aisle. We exchanged cheek kisses and stood to take stock of one another.

"Great haircut," he said.

I ran my fingers through one side. As of that morning, my hair had been shaped, textured, and highlighted, thanks be to God and Jack of Salon Noir on West Ninety-sixth. "You like it? Jack had some serious repair work after two months in the boonies."

Avi smiled. He'd bleached his teeth to a near-blue hue. "The boonies. That's cute."

I sat down in one of the chairs and gestured for him to join me. "How are you, Avi? How's business?" I thought I would proceed delicately, in case he wanted to come clean on his own regarding what Richard believed was his compromised fidelity.

He unbuttoned his light gray Euro-trim suit and lowered himself onto the velvet. Crossing one long leg over the other, he leaned back in the chair, comfortable with himself and his gleaming Bruno Maglis. "I'm well, business is very good. Too busy, but that's a good problem to have, am I right?" He smiled at me, watching my face.

"I supposed that depends on whom you ask," I said carefully. "Busy is probably as good as you let it be. Too busy and someone or something important gets neglected." My turn to peer.

His eyes held mine. He cleared his throat. "How did you feel about the rehearsal?"

Did I detect a certain snippiness in that tone? I rolled my shoulders back and forced a smile. "Fantastic. I'm excited about tomorrow. Julian has done a fine job promoting and the music will be exceptional." *If I can throw off my molasses voice by then,* I added internally.

"Right. About that," he said, shifting slightly in his seat. "I'm so sorry but I won't be able to make it to your concert. Sasha is singing at Avery Fisher and you know how difficult she can be." He rolled his eyes. "A diva among divas, if you can imagine."

I felt an uneasy prick in my stomach. Sasha Von Tassel, twenty-six-year-old chippy who had wowed audiences and critics throughout the past year as much for her impossibly large bosom and revealing concert attire as for her coloratura.

"But," Avi said, taking my hand, "I know *you* don't need me here anyway. You're the pro," he said lightly, his shoulders shrugging in deference to the crone before him.

I leaned toward him, hoping concern emitted from my eyes. "Are you all right, Avi? You seem, I don't know, distracted. Not like yourself."

"Really?" He cocked his head and made a casual search of the stage lights for an answer. "No, I feel like the old me. Maybe you're just used to your new life. You know, the slower pace." One side of his mouth edged up.

"My new life." I sighed. "Avi, why didn't you tell me about the *Pasione* tour?"

A quick shadow passed over his face but he recovered quickly. "I was still feeling out the logistics to see if it would be a good fit for you. Why? Have they contacted you directly?" He'd begun tapping one finger on his knee, the only betrayal of any nerves.

"I thought your role was to present the options to me, the one who writes your check, and then I can decide what's 'a good fit.'" I could feel my heart racing and my cheeks getting warm. "Avi, I have to assume you are trustworthy. Otherwise …"

He smirked. "Otherwise you'll find another agent?"

My breath caught in my chest. I retreated. "Let's just assume the best of each other, shall we? I, for one, have been nothing but pleased with our relationship thus far and would like to keep it that way."

"I'm doing my best, love," Avi said, the sap returned to his voice. He leaned over to kiss me good-bye. "You just get back to the city after you're done in cow country and we'll hit the ground running." He hugged me quickly and strode up the aisle to the lobby exit.

I watched the doors swing in his wake. All the orchestra members had packed up and left during my conversation with Avi. The sudden and complete silence of the auditorium disturbed me. I began gathering my things to go but stopped when my cell began to ring. I checked the number. "Unknown" blinked on the screen. I stared, letting it ring again, my mind still half-immersed in Avi's words. At the last possible moment, I answered, more out of reflex than the desire to talk with another human being.

"Hello?"

A pause, then a sonorous voice. "You coming home or what?"

My shoulders relaxed slightly. I sighed. "Mac."

"Miss Sadie. I'd appreciate it if you answered the question."

"When am I coming home?" I pulled the strap of my bag onto my shoulder and walked to a side exit. "I *am* home, Mac." My full weight employed, I pushed open the heavy door and stepped into a chilly March evening. The night sky over Manhattan struck me as artificial, like bad lighting on a movie set where the guy in charge of "stars and moon" had neglected to turn off the pale orange light of the afternoon scenes. Not even the brightest star or fullest moon could compete with the wattage illuminating this city at all hours.

"Where are you right now?" he asked.

"I'm walking south on Lexington in the Upper East Side of Manhattan."

He chuckled. "Are you kidding me, lady? I wouldn't know my upper east from my lower south. I wasn't asking for street names, just if you were in your apartment, at a restaurant, in a subway train. You New York people must assume the rest of us sit around at night poring over maps of your city."

I smiled wryly and wished I could slug him. "All right, smart aleck."

"How's this?" he said, interrupting his own laughter. He made his voice even deeper. "Hi, there, Sadie. I'm just calling from the corner of Main and Dogwood in *downtown* Maplewood, heading southwest into the feedlot district." I thought I heard him slap his knee.

I cleared my throat dramatically. "I get it. You can stop now."

Still laughing.

"People who laugh this hard at their own jokes need to socialize more," I said loudly to compensate for a bus that roared by.

"Hooooo," Mac said, coming down from his self-entertainment. "Sorry about that. See now, girl? You need to get yourself back here. I'm getting punchy about nothing at all because, as you said yourself, I need to *socialize.*" He drew out that last word in his best Barry White, suggesting a kind of socializing that a girl could get used to.

"Well," I said, more sharply than I intended. "I'll be home, *um*, back in Iowa soon enough. For now, I'm busy with this concert." I crossed the street and nearly got clipped by a cab. I scowled at the driver, who shouted something offensive regarding my mother.

"Who's talking to you?" Mac's voice had a hardened edge.

"Some insane, rabid cab driver who was raised by wolves," I shouted away from the phone and toward the disappearing cab.

"The men from your city have not impressed me with how they treat women." Mac's voice sounded gravelly. I thought I detected a sprinkling of pique in those words.

"Cab drivers have their wretches among them, just like any other profession, I suppose."

"Not large animal vets. We have no wretches."

I snorted. "Besides, do you know a fair sampling of male New Yorkers?"

"Just your agent, whose calls make you cranky, and that Richard." He stopped abruptly.

"Have mercy," I said, my voice light. "Heaven forbid you judge the men here by Avi Feldman and Richard LaSalle." I laughed at the thought. "I just happen to know some rare birds."

"Jaynie got back okay," he said, veering sharply to a different subject.

"Good," I said. "She insisted on getting to the airport alone."

His quiet laugh contrasted beautifully to the delirium drifting out to the street from a packed underground jazz club. "That Jaynie still surprises me with her stubborn streak. You'd never know it looking at her."

I stopped to look into a store window. Fantastic leather handbags beckoned me from within. My budget likely sighed in relief that the store was closed but all the much more important parts of me, like my intellect, my spirit, my unerring fashion sense, mourned the glass that separated me from the large black bag on the left.

Mac had remained silent during my episode of purse lust. I realized our lapse in conversation and was about to chime in with something witty when Mac said, "She told us about hearing you sing. In fact, we couldn't get much else out of her tonight."

"She's kind to me," I said, ever a sucker for adoration.

"Here's a sampling of her adjectives: magnificent, inspiring, and my personal favorite, spiritually moving." I could hear the smile in his voice.

"Tell her I'll cut a check when I get back."

Mac laughed and I felt a sharp pang of regret that I wasn't there to see his eyes light up. "When do I get to hear the illustrious Sadie Maddox and her 'spiritually moving' voice?"

I smiled. "I'm sure we can arrange something."

"My people should call your people?"

"For you, I'll make an exception. You can call my direct line but on one condition."

"What's that?"

"I get to pick the song."

"Ah," he moaned. "I was all ready to request 'I Like My Women a Little on the Trashy Side.'"

"That is *not* an actual song."

As punishment for my ignorance, Mac burst into the chorus.

"I'm leaving now," I said over his singing. "See you back in the land of corn."

He finished a phrase with a very awkward octave jump. The man had moxie, singing like that for a person who'd recorded with EMI. "Take care, Miss Sadie. And watch yourself around those New York wolves."

"Speaking of wolves," I said, "thank you, Mac, for calling when you did. I had a run-in with a wolf right before you called and you have redeemed what was to be a very discouraging walk home." I waved at Tom as I headed toward the elevator. "So thank you."

"You are welcome," he said, so softly I could scarcely hear him. "See you soon, girl."

I hung up and watched the lights above the elevator float down to me.

19

Network

"Sadie!" Margot Sheffield air-kissed both of my cheeks. "*Mmmwah, mmmwah,*" she intoned with each smooch. An overabundance of Chanel assaulted my nose and I struggled with the impulse to sneeze into her blonde extensions. She pulled back and held me by the shoulders. "Wednesday night. I was *there,* you were *divine,* I *adore* you."

"Thank you, Margot," I said, leaning against the wall, hoping to convey with my body language an ease I didn't feel. "I'm glad you were there."

"Would not have *missed* it," Margot said, as if the thought was offensive to her. Margot and I had known each other for many years. She came from the oldest of old money and had been my first friend among the wealthy patrons after my debut at the Met. We moved in the same circles, knew the same people, freely name-dropped each other when the occasion rose. And yet I wouldn't have called Margot a friend, mostly because I'd seen her wax and wane in her "adoration." During that exchange, for example, I chose not to mention her conspicuous absence at *Rigoletto* two summers before, the chamber series at First Presbyterian, and the Pops concert last Valentine's Day, not to mention a vicious rumor I'd suspected she'd started regarding my alleged bout with vocal nodes. Even with her indiscretions and flaky loyalty, Margot was not a person with whom I wanted to trifle. Besides, why dig up old bones, as it were, when she'd spent so much getting hers synthetically chiseled?

We were standing near the swanky bar at Deseo, me nursing a martini and Margot a gin and tonic, as we waited for the rest of our dinner party. Richard had asked a slew of people to meet for dinner the evening before I was to fly back to Maplewood. One last hurrah before returning to casseroles and cream of mushroom soup in its myriad incarnations.

Marcos and Isabel Ruiz came toward us, Isabel's slender and sculpted arms held open wide. She enveloped me in a hug and Marcos went straight to the bar.

"Sadie, you look beautiful," Isabel said. She stood at just under five feet, though she did an admirable job making up at least four inches with her impressive collection of slinky heels. "I love your dress."

"Thank you. It's perfect, isn't it?" It was true. I looked ravishing. That very morning I'd done some American Express-aided therapy in efforts to raise

droopy spirits. The blues were exacerbated by rain that
had pelted the city since the previous day. In a gem of
a store in TriBeCa, I'd happened upon the sleek black
number I wore to Deseo. Hourglass shape, tailored
from bust to hem, the dress evoked an era in which
women with curves were not only tolerated but sought
after. The overlying fabric was a peekaboo lace through
which showed a soft blonde-gold lining underneath. I
felt every inch woman, from new dangly earrings to
a pair of dangerously high Blahniks. Nothing in my
ensemble had been purchased at a discount, per se,
but I defied a woman to feel this good at fifty percent
off.

"Welcome, welcome." I heard Richard's voice before
I spotted him through the gathering crowd. "Phenomenal
jacket, Suzanne. Have you lost weight? Jules, great to see
you."

He reached my side and raised his eyebrows before
burrowing me in a hug. "Vavoom, ex-wife," he said into
my ear. "Remind me why we got a divorce?"

I pulled away and was about to enumerate a few of
my favorite reasons but a woman materialized by his side.
If she hadn't been within striking distance, I would have
assumed she were an airbrushed creation for magazine
production only.

"Sadie," Richard said, stopping to kiss the woman
on her hand. "This is Ama. Ama, meet my oldest and
dearest friend, Sadie."

"Emphasis on oldest," I muttered. Ama looked to
be no older than twenty-three. Her skin was the color of
cocoa and had clearly never known acne. A wild mane
of hair began at a high and regal forehead. I was sure

Margot would spend the next hours envying the child's cheekbones and jawline.

Ama took me in with mournful brown eyes. "Hello, Sadie," she said softly in delicately accented English. "Richard speaks highly of you." She neither smiled nor frowned, and did not betray how that observation affected her, if at all.

"Have you dated long enough to know he is a compulsive liar?" I asked, hearing the words sound more like an affront than the joke I'd intended.

"Ah, Sadie," Richard said. Ama stood at least six inches taller than he. "Let's get to celebrating you, shall we?" He spun me around by the waist and led me to a table off the main dining area reserved for us. I looked over my shoulder and saw Ama falling into line, clomping along in that bizarre foot-in-front-of-foot amble models seemed to favor.

"Where'd you dig her up?" I hissed into Richard's ear. "She's a knockout, Richard, but aren't you dabbling in the illegal?"

Richard laughed heartily. His eyes were shining in a manner I took to reflect conquest. "This is only our third date, my dear. And I assure you she is of age." He dropped to a stage whisper. "I checked her passport to make sure."

We entered the small room, lit by pillar candles lined up along mahogany shelves mounted high on the walls. More candles dotted the table. Richard turned to me, voice still lowered. "Check out the Fendi ad in *Vogue* this month. The model will look familiar to you now." He flashed me the grin of a freshman boy who'd scored a prom date with the captain of the cheerleading squad.

I took a deep breath and rolled my eyes. *How,* I wondered and not for the first time, *did I end up with my closest friend a man who had no concept of dignity?* I, the woman who still referred to a dog-eared copy of Emily Post on a semiregular basis?

"Sadie, royalty sits at the head of the table," Richard said loudly, pointing to the far end of the linen-covered rectangle. He made his way through the guests, greeting them and bossing them around. I sat and watched the filtering and seating of my group of well-wishers until all the seats were filled but the one directly to my right. I leaned over to Richard. Ama took a dainty sip of her iced water.

"Who's missing?" I asked, nodding toward the empty chair.

"You'll see." He did some sort of neck dance that made me cringe. Though I was not known for an awareness of the club circuit, I felt certain that Richard should avoid doing any sort of movement like his neck dance if he wanted to hold on to a woman/girl like Ama.

Our server brought out three *ceviche* platters and square plates of house-made tortilla wedges. I dipped into the *ceviche veracruz* and glanced at the people around the table. Mitch from St. Paul's waved and kissed me through the air. Stefan from Juilliard called out, "Sadie, have you been eating your fill of *ceviche* out in the country?" I laughed along with him but was struck suddenly with a longing for Jayne's pecan pie bars. They were indulgent, too sweet, and made with whole sticks of butter, everything a New York City personal trainer would exorcise. I adored them.

Halfway through my second martini, I had a moment of painful self-awareness: The people sharing dinner with me, those who were there to well-wish me as I returned to Iowa, these people were not my friends. I enjoyed them, sure. They liked me well enough. But they didn't know me. They wouldn't bring me tuna fish hot dish if I was postpartum, as friends of the Hartleys had done for weeks after the births of their children. And they certainly wouldn't go out of their way to fire up their pickup and bring me to work in the cold. I sighed, washed in a wave of loneliness.

In a good faith effort to enjoy my own party, I struck up friendly banter with Lyle, an arts writer for the *Times* whom Richard and I had known for years. Lyle had become animated in our discussion of the financial state of American opera when I glimpsed a familiar face at the end of the table. A woman in her mid-fifties, spiky salt-and-pepper hair and clunky, artsy glasses waved briskly to Richard and headed our way.

"… And that's exactly why the conservatories themselves have to be more comprehensive in their curricula," Lyle was saying in between shoveling hunks of *ceviche* from his plate into his mouth.

"Sorry to interrupt, Lyle," Richard said. He'd risen from the table and had an arm *near* the spiky haired woman but not *on* her. She stared at me until I felt compelled to stand as well.

"Judith, it is a pleasure to introduce to you Sadie Maddox. This is long overdue," Richard said. His eyes were unnaturally wide. I had never seen Richard intimidated by a woman but could get very used to watching a charade like this.

"Judith Magnuson," she said, offering a large, rough hand. I shook and smiled.

"I'm so pleased to meet you, Judith. Richard raves about you." I sat down slowly, willing myself not to bow down, clutch her feet, and beg her to make me one filthy rich mezzo-soprano. The woman certainly had the pedigree. I dared say even Avi would have developed a nervous tic had he known of my dinnermate that evening.

Judith unraveled her napkin and tucked it around a generous midriff. She helped herself to a dollop of the appetizer. I tried not to stare at the fervor with which she went about her task. One fleck of tortilla chip flew up into her hair and trembled there as she chewed.

We sat in silence for a moment. I glanced at Richard, who'd conveniently involved himself in deep conversation with Ama. She sat with a vacant and gorgeous stare as he pontificated on the neglected beauty of the harpsichord. I'd heard that speech and hoped it had gone through an inspired revision, for Ama's sake.

"You were magnificent Thursday night." Judith didn't look up when she spoke.

I felt my heart pick up speed. "Thank you, Judith. I didn't know you were there." *Which was best,* I thought, as the idea of her presence made me nauseous with retroactive nerves.

"That is to say," she continued, looking up briefly to meet my eyes, "it wasn't perfect. But perfect can be boring."

A compliment? An insult? *How was one to respond?* I wondered as Judith squeezed lime into her water and dropped the deflated rind into the glass. She continued before I'd formed a safe modus operandi.

"Listen. Sadie." She pushed her appetizer plate away and focused her gaze on me. "I know you're here with your friends. I don't know any of them and won't impose on your party."

"Not at all," I protested. "I'm so glad you're here—"

She held up her hand to silence me. "Thanks, but no thanks. I'm not hungry."

I reined in my eyebrow from its rocket launch upward.

"I'm here to tell you I think we'd be a good team. I've been agenting for twenty-five years. I know everyone in this business and people like me." She said these last words with all the facial and vocal enthusiasm of Ted Koppel. "If you need references, I can put you in contact with Jessye Norman, Dawn Upshaw, Jubilant Sykes. You can try Placido, but he's ridiculous about returning calls."

I tried not to salivate onto the tablecloth. This woman was my bridge to monumental, royalty-drenched, legend-making success. I worried that my heart was making visible and distracting leaping motions through the fabric of my new dress. "What a list of clients," I said, wondering if I should ask Judith for *her* autograph.

She nodded. "I've worked with the best and, if I may say so, I've gotten many of them the recognition they deserved. Now." She sat back in her chair and took a deep breath. Her eyes narrowed as they studied my face. "My practice has usually been to sign with a client at the beginning of her career. You've already been around the block. How old are you?"

Was this really crucial information? I thought. My face must have betrayed my wounded ego because Judith's expression was wry. "Believe me, if we work together, I'll end up knowing your dress size, the names of your ex-boyfriends, and the details of your monthly cycle. So 'fess up."

"I turned forty this year."

She nodded. "That can be an asset. Vocally you've hit your stride; personally you're not rudderless like so many of the younger ones; physically, you know by now that breasts aren't everything."

I sat up straight, willing them to be *something* at least.

"I'm sure Richard let you in on the *Pasione* deal?"

"He did." This was it! This was it!

"I can get you on that tour. But you'll have to dump Feldman before we talk particulars." She passed me her card and looked me in the eye. "Sadie, I think we can make each other a lot of money. Not that I need it." She shrugged. "But it's always nice to have more, am I right?" She smiled for the first time and revealed two rows of teeth that could have been shot in with a gun. I could recommend a great orthodontist as one way to spend some of her monetary excess.

Her chair scraped on the tile floor as she pushed back from the table. "Think about what you want to do and where you want to be a year from now. And then give me a call." She patted Richard on the shoulder, nodded once to me, and left the room.

Richard hopped into Judith's still-warm chair and assaulted me with questions before the spiky hair was out of view. "So? What did she say? Will she take you? Are you signing before you leave?"

I shook my head slowly. "I don't think I've ever said

so little in a conversation," I said, amazed at the way in which Judith had steamrolled our exchange. If she had that kind of sway over contract negotiations and fee schedules, the woman would be unstoppable.

"I know." Richard slumped slightly, his face taking on a look of befuddlement. "She's a *machine*."

I burst into laughter and after a moment, Richard joined me. Ama looked on from her ethereal pedestal of model-ish thought and allowed a small smile before catching herself. Good thing, considering the risk of crow's feet only two short decades off.

Three servers, clad entirely in black, entered the room with steaming rounds of *paella* and lined them up like obedient Von Trapp children down the center of the table. Richard stood, glass of tempranillo raised. He looked at me and said, "A toast."

Glasses lifted, everyone turned toward our end of the table, hushed and waiting.

"To Sadie Maddox, a woman of class, style, and infinite talent. We miss you, Sadie, we congratulate you on the new and wildly successful stage of your career that awaits you, and we look forward to your return to us from the culture vortex, the black hole, the great Midwest."

Hearty laughter sprinkled the table. I smiled as Richard kissed my cheek, lifted my glass to the group and said, "*Salud!*" That toast went down as smoothly as any I could remember.

20

Dangerous Promises

Mac met me at the airport. He sat with his long legs crossed and an arm draped along the back of an adjoining chair in a waiting area where gated passengers emptied into the main airport. He stood slowly, ball cap in hand, and watched me walk to him.

"Miss Sadie," he said, his eyes twinkling. "Welcome back."

"Thank you, Mac Hartley." I handed him my carry-on. "Are you the resident cab service here in Maplewood?"

"For you, I am," he said. He dropped my bag on a chair behind him and enveloped me in his arms. I buried my nose in his jacket and inhaled the scent of

190

him, feeling my heart beat erratically for one sweet moment. I'd given myself many stern instructions over the previous week, all of them involving not letting myself get attached to men who had intimate knowledge of cows. We were an impossible pair, I'd said to myself. It would be hopeless, a dead end, unnecessary hurt in the making. I tried retrieving the force of this argument as my nose was pressed against his chest.

"Well," I said when he released me. "That's much better than waiting for Ms. Ellsworth to show up with her clipboard."

He chuckled softly and lifted my carry-on. We walked toward baggage claim. "How was the big city?"

I sighed. "Lovely. Busy, vibrant, full of good food and interesting people."

"Why, that sounds just like *my* hometown." He smiled at me and it occurred to me he thought he was right.

♪

Two weeks later, I was fully back into the swing of Maplewood and my work at Moravia. Things at the Hartley home were revving up as spring was breaking and Cal was preoccupied with a large and risky purchase of sows. Jayne and I had lingered over tea several evenings after the kids went to bed and Cal had disappeared to tinker in the barn. We began by exulting in our New York adventure but soon drifted to stories of our childhoods, how we came to think what we did about men, God, and work. To my great surprise, I found Jayne to be a layered and thoughtful person, even with her abysmal turkey tetrazzini and questionable choice in jeans. We laughed quite a bit and I suspected we might even be friends.

In addition to my work with students, I'd been roped into serving on a faculty committee convened to brainstorm ways to reach "a more ethnically and geographically diverse student population." I had a few things to vent regarding this very topic so I'd welcomed the opportunity, though every Monday at seven when our meetings began, I questioned the depth of my altruism. Kent Johannsen served as cochair and was forever trying to embroil me in a discussion of how musical studies suffered neglect in the general college curriculum. I did my best to ignore his wild hinting for me to take up arms, unwilling to ally myself with a man who insisted on referring to his one summer waiting tables in New York as a tie that bound us together. "Of course, *you* know, Sadie," he'd say, fingering his ribbed turtleneck. "New York is just *like* that." He'd shrug and sigh happily, musing on how *like* that New York really was.

Above all, it shocked me the amount of chatter those academic types could kick up, all of it articulate and well-spoken, but none of it resolving a darn thing. I spent much of the time checking the clock on the wall and wishing they provided something more interesting in the way of refreshments than weak coffee and stale doughnut holes. Get that spectacled, bearded man on the end a little lubed up on a friendly cosmo or two, I thought, and maybe his references to the postmodern ideal in higher education would get more interesting. I'd have to keep Kent sober and turtleneck-ed, but a cocktail theme might do us well to get through to the end of the year.

My studio work spiraled into busyness as well. Several of my students were preparing senior or junior recitals, which was sapping much more of my time than I'd anticipated. Mallory, in particular, could have used more lesson time due to her abruptly intense work ethic to make her junior recital the heavy hitter of the season. I'd seen a shift in her attitude shortly after the pork chop incident. Though not quite warm, Mallory had begun speaking to me with courtesy. I suspected her new tolerance for me had more to do with my association with Mac than for my own winning nature. I myself was evidence that one could get distracted by nice teeth and infuriating charm. At any rate, Mallory was more with than against me, which was fortuitous with her recital less than a month away.

"Spin, spin, spin," I said over tied whole notes. Mallory finished the phrase and watched me for my reaction. "Better," I said, nodding briskly. "Eons better than two weeks ago. Now we shoot for amazing."

She scribbled furiously on her score and in her notebook while I described the last few touches to make the piece shine. "You're very close," I concluded. "But you can't let down for even a millisecond. If you do, the text falls, the line fades, and the audience is jerked out of the world you've created for them. Force them to stay with you in that world. Don't let them tear their eyes off you."

She wrote in silence for a moment then looked up and smiled. "I'm hoping my dress will help with that."

"*Mmm*," I said. "Do tell."

She laughed and described the dress with her hands while she talked. "Fitted bodice on the top, made of this great fabric—I'm not sure what it's called—that's gathered all around the bodice. The top is creamy white and then the bottom flares out into a ballroom skirt, chocolate brown to match my hair and eyes." She finished shyly. "I found it at this little shop in Minneapolis over spring break."

"You'll be radiant." I smiled at the girl, washed in a vivid memory of how I felt in my first recital gown. A monstrous teal number with huge puffed sleeves so beloved in the eighties—it still hung at the back of my closet in homage to the formal beginning of my career.

Mallory began gathering her things to go.

I decided to take advantage of our fragile moment of camaraderie. "Are you expecting any special attendees to your recital? Parents? Boyfriend? Long lost cousin from Walla Walla?"

Her eyes shone. "Actually, yes. My mother's coming."

"That's wonderful. Will she and your dad drive from Minneapolis?"

She snorted. "Not unless she suffers a severe brain trauma beforehand and forgets how much she detests him."

"Oh," I said, wincing. "I didn't know they were divorced."

"Since I was two," she said, a hardness creeping into her tone. "She packed up and moved to LA in search of herself. Apparently, Dad and I were an unacceptably boring part of her treasure hunt." She shuffled books and papers into a neat stack on top of the piano and busied herself loading her backpack.

"I'm very sorry, Mallory," I said. My breathing was shallow, perhaps to compensate for the deep breaths I felt the girl needed to take.

"Don't be," she said briskly. "It was a long time ago and I'm over it." She looked past me and out the window at budding trees in the quad. "She's just a very selfish person who cares mostly about her career. She's an actress, did I say that?" She pulled her gaze back to my face.

I shook my head.

"Right," she said. "She did, in fact, have all her dreams come true." Her voice betrayed all the irony that she felt. "Ever watch *Under Oath* on NBC?"

"I have on occasion," I said. In truth, I'd harbored a mild crush on the male lead, Donovan Rice, for most of my adult life.

She nodded. "My mom plays Chelsea Middleton. The redhead with a power complex and commitment issues. And they say typecasting is a myth." She looked up at me and the old, hard glint returned to her eyes. "But you're the one who knows all about fame, right? What's your take on what a successful career in the public eye can do to one's family?" She smirked, folded her arms over her bag.

I waited a moment before responding, hoping for the new Mallory to kick the old one out of my office.

"Sorry," she said quickly. "Like I said, I'm over it. We're all very civil with each other now that we're adults. And she's flying out for the recital. You know, making amends, showing her support for my interests, so on and so forth."

I exhaled, relieved that I wasn't going to have to defend my own career and pursuit of success to someone else's abandoned child. "I'll look forward to meeting her."

"Oh, you won't be able to miss her," Mallory said. She tipped her chin in thought. "Let's see if I can give you a picture … If I am Ralph Lauren, spring collection, she is straight Versace, all Donatella with regrettably little Gianni."

"*Mmmm*," I said, savoring the images. "Superbly expressed. And now I'll really look forward to seeing you two in action."

She sighed on her way out. "Never a dull moment, that's for sure." Her ballet flats squeaked all the way down the hall.

♪

By mid-April, tepid days outnumbered frigid ones. In the morning, I would yank open my blinds in the attic and see the tree below my window arching carefully toward the sky, tiny dots of green peppering its branches. The rain that farmers were so jazzed about was great for soil and things, but not so good for my hair or heels. For the most part, I was able to keep to the sidewalks, both on the farm and in town. But sometimes the need to negotiate wet concrete, pig smells, and soft earth got to be a bit much, even for a pioneer like myself.

One glorious part of spring's arrival was the light that lingered later in the day. One Friday evening, I sat by the window, watching a particularly stunning sunset drape its watercolor over the fields. When the last bit of pale yellow had faded to indigo, I stood and lay the quilt that had covered my shoulders along the back of the chair. I walked to the bathroom to wash my face. I hadn't performed deep exfoliation for several weeks, and my pores were suffering. No clean washcloths remained in the basket by the shower, so I headed downstairs. I found Jayne sitting head in hands at the kitchen table. She looked up and I could see she'd been crying.

"Jayne, what is it?" I asked, sitting down beside her.

"Oh," she said, a new well of tears spilling over. "Just part of life." She blew her nose loudly into a fresh Kleenex. From the looks of the litter on the table, she'd been through an entire box already. "My mom just called. A friend of mine from high school died in a car accident last night. Her name was Dana." Her chin quivered with the sound of the woman's name. "She has two little ones, one younger than Emmy. Cal's still not back from Bakerstown and I just want to see him …" She trailed off and then set to another loud nose blowing event, an impressive racket coming from such petite facial structure. When she'd plowed through another three tissues, she shook her head. "It's just so sad. So unbelievably sad. I'd like to help John and the kids, but they live three hours away." She gestured to her open day planner that was buried in used tissues in front of her. "I can't even find a babysitter so I can go to the funeral tomorrow."

"I'll do it," I said, shaking my head even as the words escaped my lips. *What did you just say?* I asked myself. *Please say you dreamed that part and just go back to lending a listening ear.*

Too late. Jayne turned to me, blue eyes wide and full of wonder. "Oh, Sadie, would you really? I can't tell you how much it would mean to me."

I pulled my lips back into a smile and nodded.

She threw her arms around me and crushed my trachea with her neck hug. "Thank you so much," she croaked through fresh sobs. "I didn't even think about asking *you*."

That's because doing so would be along the same lines as asking the Pope to a Madonna concert at St. Peter's Cathedral. Some worlds were never meant to meet.

Jayne looked at me, worry etched on her brow. "Not that I have any misgivings. You're so good with the children and they adore you."

That was a stretch but I was so shocked at this catastrophe of my own making that I had no words for dispute.

"I'll leave lots of instructions, if that will make you feel better." She hopped up from her chair and retrieved a thick pad of Post-it Notes from a drawer by the fridge. "Plus, you won't have to do it all by yourself. Mac can be here right after lunch, so you'll only be alone with them from six-thirty to one."

I did the math in my head. "Six and half hours," I said aloud.

Jayne was already busy documenting a short history of childrearing on her Post-its. I pulled myself up from my chair and shuffled to the door.

"Thank you, Sadie," Jayne called after me. "You're a lifesaver."

I took the stairs back up to the attic slowly, uninterested anymore in the stack of clean washcloths I'd originally sought. A lot of good they'd do me now, I thought. I didn't need a clean and moisturized face. I needed Valium.

21

The Trenches

As was my habit as least once a week, I performed Rosina in *Il barbiere di Siviglia* for a packed house at the Met clad only in my bra and rainbow-striped cotton leggings. To make things even worse, the leggings had stirrups. The audience, understandably, had a difficult time focusing, not only because of back fat and puckering in the wrong places, but also because some annoying woman kept coming over the loudspeaker intoning, "Sadie. Sadie." I twirled a few times, in beat with the music of course, trying to locate the source of my summons.

"Sadie," she said again, nervousness dripping from her voice. "I'm sorry."

I had some ideas of how the woman could rectify

the situation, one obvious measure being to retrieve my elusive costume and get me out of those tights. But each time I tried to speak, my voice became lost in thick sludge.

With dogged determination, I finally uttered a single phrase, one that has spurred many a woman on to greatness and avoidance of the embarrassment I was currently encountering: "Control top."

The sound of my voice acted as a pulley to lift my heavy eyelids and rejoin the world of wakefulness. I pushed aside my night mask. Jayne sat on her haunches, her perky freckled nose inches from mine. The room had the feel of three in the morning, deeply dark, no light escaping from the shaded windows, no sound of a house awake, only the intermittent purr of the heater kicking in.

"I'm sorry it's so early. The kids were in our bedroom by five o'clock. They're too excited about you babysitting." She smiled sheepishly and I remembered with full force my folly of the previous day.

"What time is it?" I asked, unmoving from my sprawled position on the bed. I lay on my stomach and could feel the deep wrinkles made by my pillow on a creased face.

"Nearly six," Jayne said, clearly unaccustomed to telling lies. "Um, about five-thirty-five."

I moaned.

Jayne winced. "I know, it's horrible. But," she said, her voice rising in pitch and volume, "the kids are downstairs eating their breakfast and waiting for you."

And this was the good news.

I rolled onto my side and pushed myself up with

both hands. "I'll be down in a minute," I said, massaging a kink out of my neck with sleep-numbed fingers.

Jayne crept to the stairs as if I were still sleeping. In her hands dangled two of the most sensible black shoes ever to grace the planet. I let myself fall back onto my pillow. *As if the ungodly hour weren't enough,* I thought. My wake-up call also had to involve the sting of poor fashion decisions.

♪

One hour after Jayne and Cal left the house, I still sat at the kitchen table with all three kids. That everyone was sitting at the same time represented a miracle on par with Lazarus's sudden and odorous exit from the tomb.

"Miss Sadie, did you know that there are twenty-six letters in the alphabet?" Drew's question had to navigate through a greasy bite of bacon to be heard.

"I did know that," I said. Joel bounced up and down in his chair as I poured more orange juice into his plastic cup, one he'd immediately commandeered upon ordering his beverage of choice. With the help of some valuable interpreting by his older brother, Joel had made it clear, eventually, that he preferred the Buzz Lightyear cup. As that word combination was nothing but melodic gibberish to *moi,* I had been completely lost until Drew expounded on the man on the cup, all his friends, a detailed account of the film in which they were featured, and copious amounts of editorializing on which character could "kick behind" with the greatest efficacy.

"Twenty-six letters," Drew repeated, nodding to himself. "And I know every one of them. Wanna hear?"

While Drew recited all twenty-six, forwards and then backwards, I passed out another round of Oreos. Of course I knew this was wayward breakfast protocol, but when two of the three children had cried with their mother's disappearance, I'd opened all the cupboards in a frenzy, trying to locate some coffee for my own morning needs. In the process, Joel spotted the blue package on a top shelf and when I brandished the cookies to their big mournful eyes, it was as if the sun had begun to shine right into their little hearts. Everyone became so suddenly and convincingly pleasant that I couldn't help but indulge them with the source of their joy. Five cookies each later, Emmy's eyes had begun to bulge, so I resolved to cut them off. I decided to leave the breakfast dishes, bread, cereal, and so forth on the kitchen table as the kids would likely be back for a real breakfast within a couple of hours.

"… B and A!" Drew finished triumphantly. He threw both fists in the air to exult in his brilliance but clocked Joel on the head in the process.

Joel wailed, "No hit!" His cries were as loud as an ambulance siren lodged just inside one's eardrum, only more piercing.

"Mamamamama," Emmy started in. Positive peer pressure in action.

Drew put both hands over his ears and started singing/yelling, "Crybabies, crybabies, Joel and Emmy are crybabies."

I glanced at the microwave clock. Seven-fifteen. Pale gray light made its way tentatively into the room through the window above the sink. I looked back at the trifecta of screamers.

"All right," I said in what I hoped was an authoritative voice. "No more crying."

They ignored me. In fact, Emmy upped the volume.

"Listen up!" I shouted. All three stopped kvetching long enough to look at me. Joel looked frightened, and I found it didn't bother me one bit.

"Now, you've had your Oreos and some orange juice."

"And a piece of gum," Drew chimed. He chomped to demonstrate.

"Yes. And a piece of gum for Drew."

"Gum, tooooo," Joel whined, his eyes filling with a fresh round of tears.

"Fine, fine," I said, hurrying to unwrap another piece from the pack I'd retrieved from Jayne's stash.

Drew's eyes widened to sand-dollar size. "Joel can't have gum. Mommy *never* lets Joel have gum."

My hand froze in midair on its way to deliver the contraband item. Joel's lip quivered. "Well," I said, "the rules are just a bit different today." Joel took the gum from me and giggled. "Miss Sadie isn't Mommy, she's Miss Sadie," I said, uttering a prayer of earnest thanksgiving under my breath. "But we're all done with the first round of breakfast, so how about you boys go play with your toys while Emmy stays here with me?"

"What are you going to do?" Drew asked. A wild spray of light brown hair crowned his impressive nest of bed-head.

"Clean up," I said briskly. *And then I'm going to*

curl up in the oven for the next six hours while we wait for Mac to rescue us, I thought, already calculating how many Oreos I should ration per hour to survive until then.

"Okay." Drew and Joel padded out of the kitchen in their flannel pajamas. My jaw ached watching them try to subdue the chunks of bubble gum knocking around in their little mouths.

Emmy watched me, understandably wary about her current situation.

"You're no dummy," I said as I poured myself a third cup of coffee. "You know Miss Sadie is an unfit mother."

We watched each other in silence for a full ten seconds before we heard a scream.

Joel stood in the middle of the family room, forlorn and weeping. Drew sat on the floor, racing one of their toy trucks up an arm of the couch.

"What happened?" I asked. I sat down on the carpet next to Joel. He backed up and plopped himself down on my lap. I tried to ignore the weighty feel of his urine-soaked diaper and hugged him from behind. "Drew?" I asked again.

"Accident," he said, interrupting his truck noises long enough to utter that one word.

"I'll bet," I said under my breath. Emmy began to yelp from the kitchen, where I'd left her fixed to the gooey straps of her high chair. "Drew, even if it was an accident that you used your toy as a weapon, and I must say I doubt your truthfulness here, you still should say you're sorry to your brother."

"Sorry," Drew said. He was perched along the back

of the couch like a cat. "Sorry, sorry, so sorry, banana fanna fo forry," he sang, lessening, somehow, the potency of his apology.

Joel inhaled shakily around the thumb he sucked.

"Good enough," I said. With the grace of a camel rising to its knobby legs, I rose from the floor with Joel in tow and walked toward the kitchen to retrieve Emmy. I forced myself not to look at the grandfather clock as I shuffled by. Salt in the surrogate parent's wound.

♪

Mac let out a low whistle. "How's everybody doing?" he asked, scanning our faces.

"What do you think, kids? Scale of one to ten." I gave Mac a goofy, caffeine-intoxicated grin. "It's unanimous! We're a perfect ten!" My eyes blinked at a pace unnatural to nonreptiles.

"I see," Mac said slowly. "Looks like you've had lunch."

I joined him in a survey of our surroundings. Dirty dishes from both breakfast phases, an excess of empty wrappers from something called "fruit snacks," and roughly thirty used glasses littered the area in and around the sink. At present, we sat at the table, surrounded by partially eaten peanut butter and jelly sandwiches, an empty bag of potato chips, neglected slices of apples and carrots, and the ever-present bag of Oreos. Emmy's cheeks now contained the final cookie in the package.

"Mac-Mac," Joel sang. He bounced wildly in his chair,

fueled by hours' worth of synthetic sugars understood only by nuclear physicists. I, for one, would be adding DingDongs to my diet from that day forward. So many years I'd wasted.

"Sadie?"

I came out of my partially hydrogenated fog. Mac was looking at me intently.

"Mac Hartley." I stared at him. "You're a nice looking man," I said, beaming a full smile. "Would you like some Goldfish?" I offered him the package I'd been hoarding on my lap.

"Good gravy," he muttered. He ran a hand across his face and massaged a thick patch of short whiskers. "All right. Listen up, kiddos." He walked to Emmy's chair and in one motion, pulled out the tray, unbuckled the baby, and lifted her to his arms. He turned to me and the boys. "Shoes and coats. We're going to Uncle Mac's place."

"Woo-hoooo!" The boys engaged in running circles through the kitchen, through the dining room, into the family room, and back to the kitchen. Emmy clapped her sticky hands and blew spit bubbles in Mac's arms. I watched them all from my cozy perch in the exhaustion cloud I'd rigged up for myself. *Kids,* I thought. *What a fascinating midget species.*

Mac started the gear roundup. I'd watched Jayne on many occasions as she performed this impressive ritual. In a large bag by the door, Mac placed a pile of well-loved and germ-caked blankets, an armful of stuffed animals, and a stack of story books. Five minutes in, he must have assumed I could still be trusted to sit motionless with a child and he put Emmy gingerly on my lap. He placed a small pair of purple shoes and a jacket with a daisy print on the table before us.

"Can you put these on?" he said, each word crisp and distinct as if I'd recently suffered debilitating injuries.

"Don't be silly," I said, trying really hard to be huffy but still so subdued by the morning's utter chaos that it came out sounding more like Minnie Mouse.

By the time I had both shoes on Emmy, the boys and Mac had tromped out the door to his truck. I lifted Emmy and followed, grabbing a dish towel for odor prevention on the way out. While Mac struggled to fit three of the Hartleys' SUV-style car seats in the back seat of the cab, we stood like the Clampetts waiting for Pa to tie the mattress on. I giggled into my towel, a lovely terrycloth with a rooster printed on it. The kids looked up at me curiously.

"What's so funny, Miss Sadie?" Drew asked. He appeared to be chewing on a piece of candy only slightly smaller than the size of his head. I wondered where he'd gotten it.

"Everything," I said with a shrug. "Drew, these days, everything is funny."

He went back to chomping on his cud until Mac signaled for our exodus.

22

What's In a Name

At Mac's house an hour later, Joel and Emmy were napping and Drew was coloring quietly on the floor of the living room. Mac nodded toward the front door and I went obediently, clutching my hot cup of mint tea in both hands.

"We'll be on the porch, buddy," Mac told Drew. He bent down and kissed his hair. "You're a good artist."

Drew started to smile but had to resume his tongue-out-of-mouth position to continue his work.

I pushed open the squeaky porch door and inhaled sharply. I'd been so busy with the noisy disembarkation of the children, I hadn't really noticed Mac's house. To be frank, I couldn't believe a heterosexual man had such an eye for color. The porch wrapped around his house, a two-story number painted a slate blue-gray with bright white trim. Polished copper and ceramic pots dotted the porch and front steps. Even without flowers, the pots added pretty color in all shades of patina, blue, turquoise and orange, set against a neatly painted porch floor.

I turned to my host. "You did this." I stated it as a fact.

"You'd better hope so or I've been hiding a wife in my basement." He sat down on a wide swing hanging to the far right of the front door. He leaned back and draped his arm along the top of the swing. "Come sit."

I did. We rocked in silence for awhile. I could easily imagine the porch as a welcome oasis in the middle of an Iowa summer, which, I'd been told, could put hair on the most dainty of chests.

I cleared my throat. "Thanks for the heroic rescue." I turned so I could see his face. "I'm not, *um*, used to needing help, but those three are a force unto themselves." I shuddered involuntarily in a flash of remembrance.

He chuckled quietly. "They can sure take it out of you, can't they? I think Jaynie should get an award."

"Or at least a hefty paycheck. What she endures on a daily basis, all in the name of preserving humanity …" I shook my head. "And no one even notices."

"I think Cal does," Mac said thoughtfully. "I notice. She has some good friends who are right in the thick of parenthood themselves and I'd guess they can empathize."

"Well, it's a noble profession but certainly not the

one for me," I said, setting my teacup on the porch railing. "Not in a million years could I do what she does, nor would I ever want to."

"Never say never," he said, continuing to rock us slowly back and forth.

"Nevernevernevernever," I sang in a fast trill. Mac laughed and we sat in the vibrating silence. The chains on the old swing creaked and I wondered how many times Mac had watched sunsets from his solitary vantage point.

"Mac, if I may be so bold, why *don't* you have a wife in your basement?"

His eyebrows shot up and he stifled a grin. "Typically, the women who interest me are not ones that take to living sequestered. Why? You got somebody in mind?"

I slapped him on the thigh and tried not to think about how good he looked in his jeans. "I'm serious. Why aren't you married? Good looking, smart, funny, wildly arrogant man with his own business and a flair for home décor."

"Keep going."

"Where's the wifey?"

He gave the swing a good push with his legs. "I came close once," he said quietly. He shook his head. "Just didn't work out. She was too much woman for a guy like me. Wait a minute. You know her!"

"I do?" I asked, eyebrows furrowed in thought.

He made an hourglass with his hands. "Curves that won't quit, plays the piano like a dream. You know— Norma 'Purr, Kitty, Purr' Michaels?"

It took a moment to register but I socked him on

the arm. "You sick and twisted man," I said. "I was all ready to feel sorry for you. Norma Michaels." I copped my best scolding voice. "You shouldn't joke. Norma would make this house her home in a split second. She fawns over you."

He sobered. "I don't mean to make fun. Norma's a sweet girl. We've known each other since we were kids. She's just not, ahem, my type."

"So why, again, aren't you married?"

"Tenacious little bugger, aren't you?"

"Answer the question, please, senator."

He shrugged. "I really was engaged once."

I crossed my arms.

"No, seriously. A girl I met in vet school. Her name was Maggie. We'd even reserved the church. But then," he drew a deep breath and let it out slowly. "Dad got sick and Mom needed more hands than Cal could give. So I came home a semester early and finished up from here. Maggie stayed on campus and I never saw her again." He shrugged. "She wrote me a letter, saying she'd met someone else. It was probably for the best. A person shouldn't live with a heart divided."

We rocked in silence. The sun's timid spring rays had gathered intensity in the afternoon and now shone through the budding canopy of a tree in Mac's front yard.

"I'm sorry," I finally said. "Maggie must not have been a very smart girl."

Mac looked sideways at me and raised his eyebrows. "She graduated *summa cum laude* and is making a pile of money in South Dakota."

I waved the entire state of South Dakota away with my hand. "There's more to life than that."

Mac narrowed his eyes and stopped the swing. "I'm sorry, did you misplace my Sadie? Where's the cell-phone–toting, Blackberry-obsessed, impractical-footwear girl I like so much?"

I squirmed. "I'm more than that." I was trying to soothe the wounds of this sorry bachelor and he pointed out my more shallow traits?

"I know you are," Mac said, turning to face me in the swing. His eyes twinkled. "You and Norma are the only girls for me."

I rolled my eyes. "You should cut your losses and stick to the pianist." I took a deep breath. "Just a minute—I don't think I can smell manure." I inhaled again and closed my eyes. "No poop. Just blue sky, new grass, zero pollutants, Iowa air."

"Careful now," Mac said as I lay back on his shoulder. "You could get used to it."

For the first time in my existence, I tried to picture it. Sadie Maddox, Iowan. I got stuck trying to figure out where I'd be able to procure fresh Parmesano Reggiano before it was doomed to a green canister. I did like the porch. And Mac could make a girl think twice about her bare-bones needs. But as I listened to Mac's heart beat softy through his soft cotton shirt, I felt a heavy feeling form in the pit of my stomach. I didn't want to join the ranks of *summa cum laude* girl. A heart like Mac's didn't need to be broken twice.

♪

That evening, I sat at the Hartleys' kitchen table. The light over the stove cast weak shadows over the space. The dishwasher, filled to overflowing with the day's carnage, hummed industriously in the background. Jayne and Cal were upstairs with the kids, catching up on their day with the anti–Mary Poppins and getting them to bed. I sat with my cell phone in front of me. It was fully charged and immaculately clean after my concentrated polishing efforts. I had nothing left to do but dial.

Avi answered on the third ring. "Hello." His voice dropped and I knew he'd recognized my number.

"Avi," I said timidly. I cleared my throat and overcompensated the second time. "It's Sadie." My voice sounded too loud in the empty kitchen.

"What can I do for you, Sadie? I'm just stepping out." His voice was civil but generously laced with distrust.

"I won't be long." I cleared my throat and began the speech I'd prepared. "Avi, I've greatly appreciated the work you've done on my behalf over the last several years. You are an excellent agent and I've been fortunate to partner with you."

"That will be enough." Avi sighed. "I know you're signing with Judith Magnuson. I heard over a week ago. I'm surprised it took you so long to call."

"Oh, well," I stammered. "I wanted to make sure I was making the right decision."

"You are," he said. "I'd love to make money with and for you but," he paused, "it's a tough business, Sadie. You know that."

I sat up straighter in my chair, regaining some of

my lost composure. "It absolutely is. Which is why I think we'd do ourselves both a favor to seek out different options."

"Fine," he said curtly. "I'll send you the paperwork first thing Monday. As you recall, our contract is binding only as long as both parties find this to be a profitable relationship. There will be no settlement fees."

"Thank you," I said, though I wasn't sure why.

"One more thing." The edge in Avi's voice was no longer veiled in propriety. "I want this to be clear to you: I worked my tail off trying to get your numbers back to where they should be. You're good, Sadie, but there *is* no magic formula for selling a million CDs. And as much as you might not like to hear it, in our world you are only worth as much as you sell. Even with all her talk, Judith can't make her promises come true any more than I could without people wanting to hear you sing."

My breathing became shallow. The air in the kitchen felt still and warm. I clutched the phone and searched my mind for a reply but Avi piped in again before I uttered a word.

"Expect the contract by FedEx on Wednesday." *Click.*

I kept the phone to my ear until an automaton named Claire offered to connect me to customer service. Jayne found me there, sitting motionless and staring at the yellow striped wallpaper.

She stood before me and squinted in the darkness. "Everything okay?"

I shook my head slowly.

She pulled out a chair opposite me and waited in

silence. Finally, she whispered, "I hope my children haven't done this to you."

I pulled my gaze from the wallpaper to Jayne's eyes. "I just fired my agent."

She bit her lower lip. "I'm sorry. At least, I think I am. Unless you're relieved?" Her eyebrows knit together in uncertainty.

"I don't even know," I said, shoulders slumped. "All through my career, I've felt like I'm watching a great story unfold. I've worked hard, don't get me wrong. But for the most part, I've sung well and have been lucky enough that people have paid me to do it. But now," I trailed off. "I don't know what's next, and I think I'm … scared." I surprised myself at the strength of that word but I didn't regret using it.

Jayne stared at me as I wallowed in fear and no small amount of self-pity. After a few moments, she smiled shyly. "And I thought you were going to tell me that seeing Kryptonite-green baby poop had scarred you for life."

"Well, that didn't help my emotional state." I raised an eyebrow.

"I'm so sorry," Jayne said, though she was laughing too hard to be believed. "Drew said you used an entire box of wet wipes."

"For once, he is not exaggerating." I shivered at the thought. "You're the one who should fire someone, get some better service around here."

She wiped away a tear and sighed. "Unfortunately, it's lonely at the top. The only one I could think about firing would be Cal and I like him."

I smiled. "He'd never make it without you, anyway."

Jayne leaned across the table and looked me in the eye. Hers were still teary from laughing. "Sadie, I'm over my head here with agent hiring and firing, singing careers, CD sales, and such. But," she reached for my hands, "do you mind if I do what makes *me* feel less overwhelmed?"

I remembered Jayne's enthusiastic and vocal response to the facial in New York and pulled my hands away slightly. People with that lack of verbal inhibition could be dangerous in a time like this. "What do you have in mind?"

"I'd like to pray with you," she said. Her eyes softened. "If that's okay."

"That would be nice," I said. I bowed my head and she spoke softly.

"God of grace, thank You for making Yourself available to us all the time and everywhere, even in a tiny kitchen in an old farmhouse. You are our rock, and we are grateful for someone so steadfast who listens to our prayers."

I could feel my heart pounding. Jayne's hands wrapped mine in warmth. She took a deep breath and continued.

"Your Word tells us You know us by name. You've counted the very hairs on our heads." She paused and said, "*Humph*. Well, thank You for the perspective that fact gives to everything we face, from poopy diapers to professional singing careers. We love you, God, and thank You for loving us first," she said, awe filling her voice.

I sat with my eyes closed, hot tears streaming past my eyelashes and making mascara tracks down my cheeks.

Minutes later, my eyes still closed, I heard Jayne's chair being pushed back. I felt her kiss me on the forehead before leaving me to stay where I was, basking in the warmth of a God who knew me by name.

23

Cutting Loose

The first of May announced the final stretch of classes and May Day, a curious holiday that served no purpose other than to encourage unwarranted theatrical cheeriness. When I walked by the drama building that afternoon, a group of students stood perusing a cloudy sky, debating the merits of erecting an elaborately decorated May pole if the weatherman was correct about a thunderstorm about to whip through in a few hours.

"Of *course* we should put it up," one particularly sunny coed chirped. She wore all yellow, from the floppy cotton hat on her head to striped knee socks on her feet. "Did a few clouds stop the Celtic or

Germanic tribes in pre-Christian Europe? Is this not the long-awaited dawn of spring?"

I walked on, not wishing to subject myself to Yellow's monologue. Drama majors, apparently, weren't worried about their final exam schedules, but my students certainly were. James had shown up to his lesson that morning looking like a very tall piece of oatmeal. He'd been up until four in the morning working on a physics project, he'd said.

"I had a little mishap," he said, his face showing sheepish beneath all the exhaustion. "With my boomerang."

"Your boomerang?" I leaned against the piano, arms crossed.

James nodded. "I made a boomerang and it was *perfect*. Except that I was giving it a trial run in Carmichael Hall where I have to do my presentation, right? And, *um,* it got lost somewhere in the ceiling."

I bit my lower lip. "Your boomerang got lost."

James shook his head, befuddlement all over his young face. "I can't figure it out. One minute it was in my hand and the next …" He trailed off, looking miserable.

I burst out in the joyful laughter of a person who no longer has to submit to the whims of a syllabus and then turned him to Puccini with a vengeance.

At four-thirty, I sat staring out my office window, trying to conjure up a reason to call Mac and tell him I didn't need a ride home. Since our porch talk, I'd felt myself pulling away from spending time alone with him. One look at the calendar screamed of my need to cut my tie with that man, however new and tenuous it might be. I was four weeks from heading back to New York, away from Maplewood and full throttle into resuscitating my languishing career. The semester in Nowhere, while less painful than I'd initially feared, was nothing I was looking to lengthen, certainly not for some doomed-to-fail romance with a horse vet. True, he was achingly handsome. Of course he was witty. Smart, kind, even good with children, though I couldn't see how that was important in my case. The list of perfect attributes was weighty, but when I tried picturing how Mac would fit into my life or survive even one week in New York, my spirits fell and I knew I had to make a break for it.

The view out my window had morphed into something entirely different from the first time I'd entered that cozy room. Ivy was taking cautious steps out of its buds and was busy creating an intricate green lace around the heavy glass panes. Daffodils lined the pathways of the quad below, bursts of impatient yellow and green vying for attention after so many months underground. I thought of Central Park and the way New Yorkers flocked to the largest green space in the city as soon as the weather was manageable. Oh, for a double espresso with a shot of chocolate, no cream, to sip while watching the crazy roller skaters in their spandex and sunglasses. My sighs seemed loud in the silence of the office until the shrill ring of my cell phone trumped even my theatrics. UNKNOWN blinked across the screen, explaining why the Bach fugue hadn't sounded.

"Sadie Maddox," I answered.

"Sadie, it's Judith Magnuson."

"Judith, how are you?" I said, hating myself for how eager I sounded.

"Fine. Did you sign off with Avi Feldman?"

"Yes. I received the papers in the mail and—"

"I'll send you my documents and we'll talk."

"That sounds wonderful. Judith, I'm so pleased to be working with you. I can't tell you how excited I am about this next stage, the *Pasione* tour—"

"Yes, yes, we'll discuss all that. I think you and I have the potential to do very well together." She covered the mouthpiece with her hand. I heard a man's voice in the background, then some mumblings from Judith. She returned to me, voice clear. "Sadie? I need to go. Sign the papers and call me next week."

"Okay," I said, sounding much like the yellow-clad thespian by her Maypole. "You take care now!"

There was a brief pause and then a click.

You take care now? I thought. *Who* am *I? Donny Osmond? Since when did I tell people to take care?*

I let my head fall into my hands, the sound of my breathing magnified in the little cocoon. When a girl starts telling her brand-new, bulldog agent to take care with an exclamation point, I thought, it was time for the girl to get the heck out of Iowa.

Rain sprayed underneath the tires of Mac's truck. He flipped his wipers up to the highest speed and leaned forward slightly in his seat. This was the height of bodily tension I had yet to witness in Mac's unwaveringly laid-back frame. The truck's headlights swept around a curve in the road, illuminating a wash of reflected raindrops in the falling darkness.

Mac cleared his throat. He glanced at me quickly then turned his eyes back to the road. "You're awfully quiet these days."

A semitruck roared by and gave me a moment to think of a response. I decided to try for levity. "Work has been nuts. Nothing like corralling the emotions of twenty-some stressed vocal performance majors." My laugh sounded tinny in the enclosed space. "You'd be quiet, too, if you had to mull that group over in your head."

Mac nodded slowly.

I bit the inside of my cheek and turned to look out the window.

"How's that Mallory? Still giving you trouble?"

"Not really," I said, relieved to have hooked him into the subject of work. "Her recital is just a week away. She's too preoccupied with that to bother with tormenting me."

We rode on in the sounds of heavy rain and intermittent thunder. A stripe of lightning blinded the sky above an old farmhouse.

Mac slowed the truck to a stop and turned. "Let's go to the Roadhouse tonight." I could hear the smile in his voice without turning to face him. "Sneak you out about ten?"

I shuffled a stack of papers sitting on my lap and smoothed them with my hands. "Thanks, but I don't think so. I think I'll go to bed early tonight, try to catch up on some rest." I coaxed my body into a wide yawn.

"All right, what's going on?" He shifted in his seat and clamped both hands harder onto the steering wheel. "I may be a little rusty in the dating game, but I do remember how it feels to be given the cold shoulder."

We slowed at the end of the Hartleys' drive and turned toward the house.

"Mac," I said carefully. "It's been really fun flirting with you. I haven't felt this … girly … in years. And I like you. I do."

"Flirting," he said, almost to himself as he pulled the car to a stop in front of the house. He shifted into park but returned both hands to the wheel, eyes straight ahead.

I swallowed. "But this won't work. It *can't* work."

He let his right hand drop to the key and shut off the ignition. He pulled off his ball cap and ran one hand through his hair. He fixed his eyes on my face. "Is this about Richard?"

I stopped short and then burst into laughter. "Richard?" I shook my head, still laughing. "Definitely not."

Mac looked offended. "I don't think it's unreasonable to ask. You talk to him more than I talk to any of my former flames, let's just say that."

I bristled. "Listen, while it may seem ridiculous to the average Maplewood resident, in less provincial parts of the country, it is not uncommon for people to (a) get divorced instead of suffering through decades of unhappiness and (b) even maintain friendships with their exes."

Mac shook his head and bit his lower lip. "That line is tired, all right? The whole victim complex about being among the savages for a semester? You should never have come if you couldn't muster up more respect for us than that."

A sharp rap at my window made me jump. We turned to see Jayne with Emmy on her hip. Drew and Joel hopped up and down in tandem, not very interested in keeping dry under Jayne's umbrella.

I opened the door. "Hi, everybody." I tried sounding relaxed and casual, though no one else seemed interested that Mac and I were having a heart-to-heart in the semidarkness of a rainstorm.

"Sorry to interrupt," Jayne said hurriedly. "Mac, can you come out to the barn? Cal's having some trouble with a sow."

Mac bounded out of the truck and was halfway to the barn in a matter of seconds. The boys raced after him, jumping in puddles as they went.

"You want to come?" Jayne said. She looked uncertain. "I'm pretty sure this is something you won't see in Manhattan."

"Of course," I said, suddenly flush with courage and free of the difficult conversation she'd interrupted. "I'm here for the whole experience, right?" I jumped down from the cab like a cross between Ginger Rogers and Annie Oakley. I put my arm around Jayne's waist and held onto Emmy's little leg to knit our threesome together under the dripping umbrella. "Girls," I said, "show me to the barn."

24

Birthing Pains

If the odor outside the house had accosted me to the point of trembling those first days at the Hartley farm, it was a darn good thing I'd never stepped inside the barn. I knew from Jayne and Cal's conversations that Cal spent a fair amount of time clearing out manure (pronounced *mih' nurrrrr*) from wherever hogs saw fit for bowel emptying. I stood in the shelter of the hulking building, listening to the roar of rain on the metal roof. I made it a point to take shallow breaths and wondered if Jayne would loan me her umbrella to go retrieve my air purifier out of the house. The sad truth, however, was that the place would need a purification system appropriate, say, for a fleet of Boeing jets, to even make a dent in the problem.

The building stretched long and low, stall upon stall filled with plump and snorting pigs. The sheer size of the place dizzied me. These animals were living in an edifice that, in terms of square footage, would make Donald Trump's skin tingle. We were talking at least one city block, all devoted to ham and bacon in the making.

Jayne hung her umbrella on a hook by the door and motioned for me to follow her. I'd decided against my Jimmy Choos that morning, what with the afternoon forecast, and had opted for a cute but flimsy espadrille. The soles were made of cork and I feared they were no match for the walk to the barn. I tiptoed behind Jayne toward where the men and children stood.

"… So we'll have to help pull," Mac was saying. He stood over a huge and heaving animal that lay on her side between him and his brother. Mac cleared his throat when he saw me reach the edge of the group.

Cal looked past Jayne to me. His eyebrows shot upward. "Miss Sadie, this might not be the best time for a barn tour."

Mac ran a hand across his mouth in an effort to hide a smile.

I stood as tall as I could, pulling my chin up as I straightened. Unfortunately, the fence or whatever that surrounded the men and squealing pig was unusually high and my good posture merely positioned my nose above the top rung. "Don't worry about me, boys," I said, sure I was evoking the bravado of Laurey in *Oklahoma*. "I'll be fine watching from over here."

Cal glanced at his wife. She turned to me and put an arm around my waist. "Are you sure about this?" she said into my ear. "This kind of thing can get a little hairy."

"Ha, ha!" I said like a magician at the end of his trick. "Even *I* know a baby pig's not hairy. Get it?" I scrunched my nose, gay and lighthearted as any farm-bred, good old Iowa girl. "I am certainly not afraid to witness one of life's miracles."

Cal shook his head slightly. "Suit yourself. Kids, go stand by your mother."

Joel and Drew scampered over to Jayne and climbed the fence to have a better view. Emmy had a toy in each hand and hit herself hard on the head with a plastic reproduction of the Cookie Monster. She began to wail and Jayne looked at me, exhaustion registering on her face.

"I think I'd better put her to bed," she said. "Are you okay here without me?" Jayne swayed and bounced back and forth as Emmy's cries got louder.

"Absolutely," I said, trying hard not to roll my eyes. What did these people think I was, anyway? An incurable prima donna? I'd made it through Met auditions three times without one tear shed. They did not know the depths of my strength.

"Okay." She looked entirely unconvinced. "Boys, stay back here by Miss Sadie, all right?"

Joel bounced up and down on his perch. Drew nodded without taking his eyes off the sow.

"I'll be right back," Jayne said and hustled toward her umbrella and the door. Emmy's cries became absorbed in the cacophony of rain.

Mac turned from a small table in the corner of the stall. He wore long gloves and was spreading a goopy substance onto them, all the way up to his shoulders. He caught me watching and said, "Good, old-fashioned dish soap." He didn't smile, just returned to the task at hand. I felt my heart drop, so accustomed was I to his warmth. I turned my gaze deliberately from Mac and looked down at the pig.

Her sides heaved and though I was no expert in interpreting the intricacies of pig body language and facial expressions, I was willing to bet she was miserable. Beyond miserable, pushing straight on into desperate, maniacal, perhaps even suicidal. I certainly would have been, considering what she was enduring.

"How many babies are in there?" I asked Cal, watching her mammoth belly rise and fall. The longer I watched that animal breathe, the more adrenaline coursed through my system. Her girth struck me as something not fit for drawings of Noah's ark. Hapless children in Sunday school would never get over the image and would swear off church and Bible stories forever.

Cal pulled off his hat and tossed it to Drew, who proudly donned it and smiled at Joel. Joel's lip started to tremble but Mac saw the exchange and tossed his own cap to the younger brother. Mac winked at the boy, looked at me and turned away.

Cal stood with his arms crossed, still pondering the glories of hog reproduction. "Sows can have anywhere from seven to fifteen. I'd guess this one will have ten or eleven in her litter."

I nodded and gulped. I wasn't very good at sharing my bathroom much less sharing my uterus with ten squirming beings. I shuddered and tried to think of what *Oklahoma* Laurey would do if Curly shared a pig birthing with her, sometime after "Oh, What a Beautiful Mornin'" and before "The Surrey With the Fringe On Top."

Mac kneeled at the pig's head and talked quietly to her. What, now he's the Pig Whisperer?

"What's he doing?" I asked Cal softly.

"She's a gilt, which means this is her first birth. The first of the litter is sitting breech and she can't get it out. Mac's trying to calm her because she's a bit riled up."

I nodded, feeling a tad guilty for thinking Mac was trying to be Robert Redford. I supposed I would need a good talking-to (and preferably a record-breaking epidural) were I about to birth ten or eleven children and the first one sideways.

Cal went to hold the pig at her shoulders, though I didn't see her trying to run anywhere. Mac stooped down at her less attractive end, where we had box seat views. "Ready?" he asked Cal.

I looked nervously at the boys, standing beside me. Joel was hanging backwards by his legs and then flipping over onto the floor before starting the acrobatics all over again. Drew was watching his dad and uncle, chomping on a wad of gum and looking only mildly interested.

"Should they be here?" I asked Cal.

He looked up, distracted, and nodded quickly. "Seen it plenty of times before. Go ahead," he said, eyes on his brother.

Mac took one lubed-up arm and stuck it right up into that pig, whose yelping was only a fraction of what I would have done. I caught my breath and clutched one hand to my chest. Mac moved his arm around in there for what seemed like an eternity, though we should really ask Ms. Gilt if we want to start supposing. After he'd exhausted his real estate, Mac grunted and said, "I think I've turned him around. Here's the pull."

With a gush of liquid I'd prefer not to describe, out came a miniature version of the poor mother, likely confused and disgusted with this first experience of the rest of his life. Then out came another. And another, all goopy-ed up and shining with blood. I saw a few pigs start to spin around each other, and then one of them started to sing a tune from the Beatles' White Album. Sometime around the first chorus, I felt Jayne's arm around my waist and heard her say, "Sadie, are you all right?"

I nodded and smiled before my knees buckled and the room went black.

"Moo shu bibbity bobbity boo," said a deep voice above me. "Partridge in a pear tree."

With great effort, I opened my eyelids and saw his face hovering over mine. I closed my eyes again. "Are you ordering *moo shu*?" My head was throbbing. "There's no good *moo shu* in Maplewood."

Mac laughed softly. "There she is," he said.

I opened my eyes again and trained them on Mac's. "Your house reeks."

He shook his head, a broad smile on his lips. Such nice lips. "We're in Cal's barn. You were watching me pull a pig and—"

I groaned and raised one hand. "I remember, I remember. Please." I shuddered. "Am I going to be all right?"

Jayne popped into my line of sight. Her eyes shone with tears. "You'll be fine." She patted my arm and helped Mac raise me slowly to a sitting position. Apparently Mac had washed up a bit. "I just feel horrible, that's all. I never should have invited you to come with me into the barn." She brushed a tear off her cheek.

"Nonsense," I said. I put one hand up to my head and held it there. "I came willingly. Apparently, I'm more delicate than I'd thought."

"There are plenty of people around here who wouldn't be up for dish soap arms, even if they've been on a farm their whole lives." Mac brushed a strand of hair off my forehead. I swooned, but it might have been the aftereffects of passing out onto a concrete barn floor.

Jayne sat very still, her eyes big and watchful as Mac brushed the hair off my forehead with one gentle hand. She threw a glance to Cal. He watched his brother as if encountering a rare animal in the zoo. Jayne cleared her throat. "Cal, boys, why don't we head into the house and give Miss Sadie a moment to herself. I mean, with Uncle Mac. Together. Just the two of them." The color in Jayne's cheeks had returned and was blossoming to full glory. She stood and brushed off her jeans. Cal helped her shepherd the boys out of the barn amid Drew's protests that they be able to stay and "watch Miss Sadie fall down again."

Mac sat quietly beside me. We faced the yawning barn door, open to the rain falling in sheets outside. A flood of cool, clean air swept through the barn. I felt exhaustion seep through me.

"Here's the thing," Mac said. His voice was low and calm, bringing to mind Barry White and a hot toddy.

"First of all, I'm glad you're okay." He leaned toward me and brushed my cheek with a kiss. I tucked my face down into his neck and felt it warm me. He pulled away gently. "And as for what we were discussing earlier."

I gulped. For being such an extrovert in my profession, I was turning into quite the ninny when it came to addressing conflict with cowboys.

He smiled so sweetly I thought he might kiss me again. "I don't like getting dumped." His smile fell.

I winced.

"But I've waited a long time to meet you, and we're not done."

I started to protest. "Mac—"

"That's all right," he said, shaking his head. "You've said your piece and I respect that. Don't worry, I won't start hanging around the attic or sending suspicious packages or anything." He drew up his knees and rested his hands on them. "But the Bible says that God has a plan for us, that it's a plan to prosper and not to harm us, a plan to give us hope and a future." He rose to his feet, brushing dirt off his rear. "And whether you feel good about it or not, Sadie Maddox"—he helped me up and let me lean on him as we walked slowly to the door—"you're a part of the plan." He smiled at me sideways.

I sighed deeply. Where *was* I, a tent meeting? Church of the pig pullers? This man was just not *getting* it. "Mac, I don't even know what to say."

"Now, there's a first," he said. He held me tight as we walked carefully through the rain toward the light on the porch.

25

Performance Art

"Are you sure?" Jayne's eyes betrayed hurt.

"Yes," I said, hugging her. "These last weeks of the semester will be crazy and I should be closer to campus. I can't imagine the folks at the Maplewood Inn could be as wonderful as you all, but I'm sure they'll take great care of me."

"All right," she said reluctantly.

The Saturday morning had arrived in a burst of celebratory sunshine after a week's worth of rain. Cottony clouds paraded through a cheery blue sky. We stood in front of the Hartleys' porch, which was freshly swept and looking forward to ample traffic in the coming warmer months. Jayne squinted into the sun, which was already arching away from the horizon behind me.

I leaned over to kiss Emmy, who jostled on Jayne's hip. "Tell your sleepyhead brothers I said good-bye but that I'll still see everybody at church."

Emmy squirmed to be put down onto the dew-kissed grass.

I pulled the handle out of my Louis Vuitton carry-on. Cal hefted both of my suitcases and I trolled behind him to the truck. In the days following our talk in the barn, Mac and I had made a valiant effort in our commutes back and forth from town. His calm assurance that we were merely in a holding pattern had first annoyed and then worried me. I decided the best option was one of avoidance. Mac clearly wasn't catching my drift and I wasn't about to go through the whole thing again. I'd called the Maplewood Inn the previous night and rebooked my reservation through the Monday after graduation.

"Change is good," I said, smiling shakily at Cal when I realized I'd spoken my thoughts out loud. *Besides,* I thought, *there's nothing worse than leading a man on when there's no hope for a future together.* I slammed the passenger door shut for emphasis.

One week into my stay at the Maplewood Inn, I had the knots in my neck and back to prove it. Without Dr. Glenn, the most sought-after chiropractor on the

Upper East Side, I was at a loss of how to get my spine adjusted back to a straight line instead of the mess I'd created for it by sleeping on a glorified cot. My room at the Inn, though impeccably clean, offered none of the comforts of home. The bedspread was a flimsy nylon number splattered with a floral pattern that made my head hurt. It was fortuitous that I'd come prepared with my own shampoo, conditioner, and other necessities, as the Maplewood Inn had not been informed of the national trend toward complimentary toiletries in hotels. I felt lucky to have a clean towel every day. Each morning as I got ready in the fluorescent-lit bathroom, I'd garner all my exasperation at the pathetic accommodations, readying myself to approach the front desk with my complaints. I *wanted* to lay into the owners, Mr. and Mrs. Shipley. But all my resolve would vanish when Mr. Shipley would stand from his chair behind the desk and call out a chipper, "Very good morning to you, Ms. Maddox. And how'd you sleep?"

Mrs. Shipley would scurry from the small sitting area where she provided a "continental breakfast," consisting of Wonder Bread, watery Folgers, and a basket of waxy apples. "Morning, Ms. Maddox," she'd say, cheeks pink and eyes twinkling even at that fragile hour. She'd shuffle over to me and hand me a cup of that dreadful coffee, poured especially for me into a Styrofoam cup. "Just a little something to start the day out right," she said, without fail, each time acting like spontaneity and wit had just taken hold of her—she couldn't help herself.

"Thank you, Mrs. Shipley," I would say, swallowing

the bile of my woes and resigning myself to yet another night's sleep under nylon flowers.

I *had* to get back to New York. My spine, figurative and literal, was deteriorating under the pressure of all that midwestern *nice*. The inability to be my own advocate didn't stop with the spartan accommodations. That Sunday, two weeks to the end of the school year, I'd acquiesced to Norma's unrelenting requests for "special" music. We'd met at the church after Wednesday evening's choir rehearsal. I'd insisted that I pick the piece, much to her chagrin, as she'd had in mind something by a group called the Sweet Jesus Five that involved not one, not two, but three glissandos up and down the length of the keyboard. She wanted to be Yanni, for Pete's sake. I stood firm through her requests and her pouty lower lip and provided the piano accompaniment to a simple but lovely arrangement of "Amazing Grace." During our rehearsal that evening, it took a great force of will to ignore Norma's wild gesticulating at the piano. The woman must have had some close calls with neck injuries. But by that time in my week, my semester, my life, I was out of energy to discuss the finer points of musical performance.

I wasn't looking forward to church at all, much less my musical debut at Calvary Baptist. Jayne had dropped by the hotel earlier in the week with a basket of rhubarb muffins. The gesture was so thoughtful and so much better than Wonder Bread, I'd thought I would burst into tears. Instead, I'd overcompensated in trying to remain detached, which resulted in a cold reception. I hadn't wanted to, but I knew I'd hurt Jayne's feelings. She'd left quickly and I hadn't heard from her since.

Mac had left a slew of funny and endearing messages on my phone, all of which I'd saved but none to which I'd responded. His final voice mail was notably sharper in tone. I suspected his God theory was beginning to show holes and he was finally getting the idea that I was moving on, moving up, moving out. The whole Hartley clan was sure to be at church on Sunday and my goal was to avoid eye contact with every one of them as I sang four verses of the hymn.

My one consolation that morning was my new Chinese brocade silk jacket. The fit and fabric assured me I could justify every dollar I'd paid at that chichi spot in Midtown during spring break. My hair shone in the spring light as I stepped out of my luxurious hired transportation. Unbeknownst to many, Maplewood did, indeed, have one lone taxicab. Driven by a slovenly but blissfully quiet man named Tom, the cab looked a lot like my mother's old station wagon from the early seventies. Mustard yellow with wood paneling, I'd cringed the first time Mr. Shipley had waved the wagon toward the front entrance of the hotel. Though Tom himself could have used a few pointers on personal maintenance, the car shone inside and out with clean windows, seats, and floor mats. Equally redemptive was Tom's tomblike silence, other than an embarrassed announcement of the fare at the end of each ride. Our soundtrack was the hum of the road beneath us and the public radio station, tuned to a soft drone of Mahler, Beethoven, and Grieg. Sure beat Mac's "My Girl's Got Childbearing Hips" on the country dial.

"Ooooo, what a snappy jacket!" Even from across the

sanctuary, I could see Norma's nose pinch in a scrunch of delight. "It's so *exotic*."

"Thank you," I said, though not entirely sure of the compliment. "You look snappy too." I took in Norma's outfit: lime green blouse that ballooned in decorative poofs down her arms, tropical print capri pants in a sturdy polyester, and flip flops crowned with large pink rosettes near painted toenails. Snappy.

We ran through the piece twice before Norma flew to the small portable organ to begin a rousing Bill Gaither medley for prelude. I sat in the front pew and studied my bulletin as parishioners trickled in from the lobby. A few minutes before the service was to start, Drew and Joel Hartley came rushing up and nearly toppled me in a joint hug. Jayne hurried behind.

"Miss Sadie, we miss you," Drew said, not unlike a line in a school play. "Joel," he whispered loudly and gave his brother a generous nudge.

Joel looked at Drew a moment and quickly produced from behind his back a mangled bouquet of peonies. He smiled at me and thrust them forward.

I took them from his sweaty hand. "Thank you, boys. Your mom is raising two little gentlemen." By the time I finished my sentence, they'd run off to join their dad in the Hartley pew.

"Sorry about the attack," Jayne said. She leaned down and hugged me close. I could smell her raspberry shampoo and the fresh scent of dryer sheets. "We *do* miss you, you know." She smiled and her eyes said nothing of hurt feelings, just the truth of her sentiment.

"I miss you too. God bless the Shipleys, but I'm losing weight by the day. One can only stomach the soup and salad bar at Old Country Buffet so many times."

She giggled. "True, but you're smart to stick to the soup and salad. I worked there during high school and haven't been back since."

I sighed. "I should just walk up to the square to eat at Marv's."

"No," she said gently, "you should just make up with Mac and move back to our place." She watched my face. "Pancakes every morning," she said hopefully.

I patted her knee. "So you've talked with Mac."

She nodded.

"Mac, as you know, is a wonderful man," I said. "But he and I live in different worlds. It can't work." I sat up straighter, willing myself not to search the congregation for his face. "I'm sure you understand."

"I'm sure I don't," Jayne said, her tone wry but playful. "But you're grown-ups and I can't give you two a time-out, so I'll have to settle for a bouquet of peonies." She gave me a quick hug as Norma tumbled toward a dramatic close to her medley. Jayne hustled down the aisle and toward her family and I settled in to wait for my cue, the offertory prayer.

While the pastor blessed the offering, I tiptoed up carpeted steps to the small stage. Norma flashed a thumbs-up from her seat at the piano. I stood in the curve of the Baldwin and looked out on the congregation. Mac caught my eye above all the bowed heads. His face had the glow of an early tan, which stood out nicely against a pressed white button-down. He winked at me, a shy smile forming on his lips. I shook my head slightly and his grin widened. I bowed my head and waited for the end of the prayer.

It wasn't until the middle of the second verse that my eye accidentally swept toward the Hartley pew again. Jayne was holding Joel, her cheek on his. Cal sat forward in the pew, his face inscrutable but probably hiding thoughts of hog prices. Mac sat motionless, with an expression of surprise on his face. I realized this was the first time he was hearing me sing. *Just goes to show,* I thought. *The man has never even heard my voice, much less a set of Strauss songs or an entire opera.* Of course, I hadn't exactly volunteered to accompany him to a cow surgery, or whatever it was that he did. In either case, we were two ships, wrapping up our pass in the night and ready to return to our lives as they were meant to be.

My gaze left Mac and traveled onward through "many dangers, toils, and snares," and right into ten thousand years of singing. Spontaneous applause erupted when I'd finished. I thought Norma was going to kick off her rosettes and do a holy shimmy, she looked so pleased. I smiled at the pastor as I passed and he wiped at the corners of his eyes.

"Thank you, Sadie," he said into the microphone over the podium. "I can't imagine a more beautiful sound than that of God's children singing together for eternity, amen?" Amens resounded and I smiled from my seat in the front. "As long as we all can sound less like me and more like Sadie Maddox," he added, chuckling along with his congregants. It was true. The man's voice cracked liked a sixth grader's. To prove his point, he led us in congregational singing of the first verse of "Amazing

Grace" and I think we all agreed second time was not a charm.

After the service, I stood near the front of the church and accepted the kind compliments of many Calvary Baptist attendees. At the end of the line stood Mac, which caused me to draw out a conversation with Norma far beyond what was reasonable. She was neck-deep in a story about her nephew who was studying the harp at the University of Iowa but was hoping to transfer to Juilliard and did I have any contacts, when she noticed my eyes flicker to Mac behind her.

She turned and gasped. "Mac Hartley, why on earth didn't you tell us you were standing there?" She took a deep breath, wallowing in his tan and other fine attributes. She lowered her voice to what I think was an attempt at Saucy Norma. "We girls will talk the day away without a man to distract us."

Nose scrunch for Norma.

Vomit danger for me.

"Might I have a word?" Mac asked Norma, nodding toward me.

"Of course," Norma said. She looked slighted but bounced back quickly. "I'll be in my office if you need me." She smiled up at Mac. "Either of you." She and the tropical booty swished away.

"Sadie," Mac said, stepping closer to me and then back again. "I, *um.*" He sighed. "Geez. This is ridiculous. Listen, I just want to tell you that I've never, ever heard someone sing like that." He gestured toward where I'd stood by the piano. "It was … ethereal."

I raised my eyebrows. "Big word for an animal vet."

He shook his head, ignoring me. "God's blessed you something fierce."

"Thank you, Mac." I looked down, blushing in spite of myself. Very seldom in my line of work did one get to see such unabashed appreciation, no strings attached. "I wish the music industry felt as strongly as you do."

He shrugged. "Why does it matter what they think?"

"Well," I sputtered, "they're the ones who control my income. They butter my bread, so to speak."

"Not really," he said. "If God can take care of the lilies, I think He can handle a feisty soprano. Even one with commitment issues."

"Cute," I said, turning to gather my things on the pew. "I appreciate your pithy sayings, Mac, but the point, *again,* is that we don't understand each other."

"That's funny," he said. He'd planted himself in front of me and was making no effort to let me pass. "I see it more that we understand each other perfectly. So perfectly, in fact, that it scares you."

I scoffed. "It *scares* me?" I said, a little too loudly because a rowdy group of high schoolers talking near the back turned to watch. I lowered my voice. "What are you now, Dr. Phil?"

"Close," he said, grinning. "Dr. Mac. Hey, that has a nice ring to it. Dr. Mac, relationship consultant."

I shook my head in exasperation. "I have to go." I pushed past him, gently so as not to be the reality show for the Calvary Baptist youth group.

He pulled me back toward him. Before I could push back, he leaned down and planted one right on my lips, right in front of a gaggle of open-mouthed freshman girls. He pulled back quickly and said, "I know you do, dang it." And then he strode past me and up the aisle. His posture was brooding but he still gave a high five to a grinning boy on his way out.

If I'd been a preschooler, I would have stomped my foot and huffed. I had to settle for an internal huff as the teenyboppers were watching for their next installment. I lifted my chin and walked ceremoniously out of the sanctuary, poised and lovely in my silk and inwardly thinking, *Two. More. Weeks.*

26

The Show Must
Go On

Mallory rolled her head slowly in an arc from shoulder to shoulder, attempting to loosen the muscles in her neck. The soft lighting in the green room of Moravia's Great Hall contrasted sharply with the stage lights she was readying herself to face.

"You look exquisite," I said, admiring the fresh, young face. Her expression betrayed a bit of anxiety but mostly excitement for her junior recital. "And it's not just the dress, although you were right about that, too."

Her eyes shone, luminous and warm with shadow

and liner. The dress she'd raved about made her look every part the sophisticated professional. I was pleased, considering I'd seen my share of bad prom dresses on this very stage during the last few weeks of year-end performances. A curvaceous soprano the week prior had glided onstage in a full-length sequined fuchsia gown, low cut and trimmed with feathers. I hadn't heard a single note due to the strobe-light effect every time the girl moved.

Mallory smoothed her pleated bodice and rested her hands on an impossibly small waist. "Thank you." She sang a rapid scale on *mi*. "I can't believe I'm this nervous."

"Happens to the best of us."

"Really?" Her eyes widened, temporarily distracted from her own woes.

"Absolutely," I said. "I spent the first ten years of my career downing anti-anxiety medication before each performance. Don't even get me started on how many *very famous* people, who will remain nameless, rely on everything from hypnosis to Vicodin to get through the stress of performing."

She let out a deep exhale. "I think I'll run to the restroom. It's what—ten minutes to curtain?"

"Take your time. Walk slowly and like you're not one bit nervous. Lots of times the body can persuade the mind."

"We'll see," she said. She walked carefully to the door and slipped out.

I was sitting on the couch, nursing my chilled spring water with lemon, when the door flew open and Mallory scurried in. She shut the door and blocked it with her body. Her shoulders heaved.

"I never should have looked," she said. Her eyes filled to brimming with tears that spilled over in a hasty exit.

I jumped up. "What? What's wrong?"

Her pretty makeup forged muddy black inlets down her cheeks and chin. I looked around frantically for a towel to bib the girl. That cream bodice was not mascara-proof.

"She isn't here. I knew it. I just *knew* it." She slapped her hand against a nearby wall for emphasis and then winced with the pain.

"Come sit," I commanded, glancing at the clock. Whatever this girl was talking about had to be resolved in quick order. Sounds from the quickly filling auditorium filtered through the stage door. "What happened?" I ushered her over to a small sofa by the window.

She sniffed and made a noise incongruous with the image I'd so enjoyed before she'd left the room. "My mother," she said, already sounding nasal. "My self-absorbed mother is not here. I saw my dad in the hallway and I could tell by his face." She took the tissue I held out to her. "He said"—she paused to blow—"he said she called to ask for my address to send a dozen roses. Can you believe that?" A fresh wave of tears fell down her cheeks. "She wants to send roses instead of coming to the single most important night of my life but she doesn't even have her own daughter's address."

I pulled her to me. "I'm so sorry, Mallory." She wept on my shoulder, which I'd preemptively covered with my shawl in case of snot. "People can be heartless, even people we love."

She sniffled on my shoulder for a few moments and then sighed deeply. Her shoulders trembled with the release of tension. "I can't do this."

I shifted in my seat and gently nudged her to face me. "Yes, you can."

She shook her head. Her lower lip trembled. "I can't. I don't even want to."

"Now, just a minute," I said in my newly acquired professor voice. "You have worked tirelessly the last few months to prepare for this evening. Not to mention all the years of preparation it took to get to this point. The lessons, the exams, the smelly practice rooms." I wrinkled my nose and she risked a small laugh. "You cannot let a woman who is not willing or ready to recognize your worth destroy what you've worked so hard for." I swallowed hard, suddenly and unfortunately hit with the similarities between the hurt I saw in Mallory's eyes and what I'd seen in Mac's that Sunday. "Believe me. Speaking as a person well-versed in the art of self-absorption, you shouldn't let people like us ruin your day."

She shook her head. "You're not like her. She never knew the right thing to say."

Well. Now. That was a first. Sadie Maddox, knowing the right thing to say.

I glanced at the clock. "We have three minutes." I reached for my purse and unloaded a heap of cosmetics on the small coffee table in front of us. I looked her in the blotchy red eyes. "Ready?"

She closed her eyes and took a deep breath. When she opened them again, they were clear and determined, much like the day I first saw her in the choir room. This girl was going to be a force, whether her mother acknowledged Mallory's brilliance or not. I hoped she would come to her senses before Mallory closed the door for good.

"I'm ready," she said and made her face a blank slate for my powder.

Mallory shone that evening. She sang the baroque selections at the beginning with poise and elegance. The German *lieder* became progressively more passionate, and by the finale—a heart-wrenching aria from Floyd's *Susannah*—my cheeks were stained with the tears of a proud teacher. Mallory called me up onto the stage after her encore, a comedic number from a favorite musical. I hugged her fiercely and said into her ear, above the applause, "I have never been more proud."

She grinned and kissed me on the cheek. We faced the audience, hand in hand and soaking up the sweetness of the moment. Right before we bowed together, I saw a tall man in the back rise from his seat, don a ball cap, and slip out the door.

Ellsworth's clanking but reliable Camry coasted to a stop in front of the sign reading *Departures, All Airlines*. I sat with one hand on the door handle, still amazed at the virtual absence of human traffic in the Maplewood Airport. I heard some quiet sniffling and turned to see

Ellsworth reaching for a Kleenex from a crocheted box on the dash.

"I'm sorry," she said, blotting her eyes. She blew loudly into the tissue but her perm remained strangely unmoved. "I'm not very adept at good-byes."

I reached out to pat her arm, which brought about a new wave of tears. "You've been very kind to me, Ms. Ellsworth, and I will always appreciate that."

She drew in a long, shaky breath. "Of course, this isn't good-bye forever." Her smile revealed a smudge of coral lipstick on her front teeth. "The dean said you'll consider being a part of our concert series next year, is that right?"

She looked so hopeful and that lipstick was so pathetically Merle Norman, my nod was decisive. "Absolutely. Just remind Dean Johnson to call my agent. I'll e-mail you her contact information."

"Wonderful. Now, that is *wonderful*." Ellsworth extracted another Kleenex from the box and folded it once before dabbing at her wet eyes. "Well, Miss Maddox, you have been a delight to have on campus. I wish you all the best." The last sentence was nothing short of a squeak. Ellsworth threw herself at me across the middle console and wrapped me in an awkward but determined hug.

"Thank—thank you, Ms. Ellsworth," I said, coughing to relieve the pressure she was putting on my neck. She relented and I patted her back in gratitude. She inhaled a few of those convulsive breaths one has to endure after tears have subsided.

"No," she said. She pulled away but kept her hands on my shoulders. "Thank *you*. Our students simply glowed after spending time with you. Especially Mallory Knight."

I smiled at the thought of Mallory, the student I'd first thought most qualified to inspire an Aaron Spelling television series but who ended up showing me why people languished on in the field of education.

"She's applying to Juilliard, Eastman, and Curtis for vocal performance. Did she tell you?"

I felt my heart surge and my eyes widen in pleasant surprise. "No, she didn't. But I'm very, very pleased." I watched a mother and her small child cross the street and giggle as they turned in the revolving door. "I wouldn't say it about many people, but Mallory will be able to make a career out of her singing and do it well."

"She was lucky to have you come along at just the right moment. The day before you arrived, she was headed to the registrar to change her major to accounting."

I laughed. "I'm glad I got there in time."

Ellsworth turned to me abruptly. "Well. I'll help you with your luggage." She bounded out of the car, black pumps in motion, and popped the trunk. We wrestled together to get my two suitcases into standing position on the asphalt.

I hugged Ellsworth gently and quickly, said a cheery good-bye and pulled my gear toward the check-in. It occurred to me that four months before, when I'd looked at Ellsworth, I had seen merely a bad perm, worse shoes, and a sequestered midwesterner in need of an urban experience. That final morning in Maplewood, though, I knew the sinking feeling in my chest was one of genuine affection—for Ellsworth, for my students, and quietly but stubbornly refusing to go away, for a veterinarian whom I hadn't called to bid farewell.

"Destination?" The redhead behind the counter continued typing madly on the black keys before her. Her eyes had not left her computer monitor. Apparently, airline behavior was standardized across time zones.

I stood for a moment, lost in thought.

"Ma'am?"

I focused on the redhead's face. She waited, hands poised above the keys.

"LaGuardia Airport, New York City."

27

There's No Business

The sound of my three-inch strappy summer heels clicked through the otherwise empty corridor. I took a deep breath, trying to calm my heart rate after a particularly hectic morning. Four months in Maplewood had numbed me to the fact that getting places in New York required an amount of time defying spatial logic. I'd been back in the city for three weeks and was gradually finding my way back to my old routine. After two meals at Jasmine, daily trips to my beloved grocery where I purchased four types of hard cheeses from Holland, and a ballet at Lincoln Center, I was feeling at home once more. Some things, though, had taken a bit of acclimation. The caking of city grime on my face and feet caused a twinge of longing for the clean—though pig-infused—air of Iowa. The complete lack of silence at any time of day, in any part of the city, was an adjustment I hadn't anticipated. I'd taken up scouring menus and grocery stores for a *real* pork chop. And the need to leave one's apartment an hour before an appointment, even if the meeting place was less than a mile away, had caused me to be late to the first meeting of the rest of my career.

While still in Maplewood, I'd received from Judith a broad outline of the schedule for the *Pasione* tour, beginning with that morning's initial meeting. Judith and I had been playing a very long game of phone tag since I'd come back to New York, but I hadn't worried, as I knew I'd see her at that first meeting. I stopped to powder my nose and reapply my lipstick when I came to the closed door of the conference room. I could hear muffled conversation from the other side. I smoothed my skirt, fluffed my hair, and turned the knob.

My eyes swept the room, taking in the singers, noticeable for their colorful wardrobe choices and their dramatic speech mannerisms. Interspersed among the singers were dark and stuffy suits and dresses draped on agents. I scanned these and found Judith at the end of the table, sandwiched between two pretty girls, one with dark short hair and the other with a long curly blonde mane. The blonde nudged Judith when she saw me striding toward them, smiling and feeling the world was my new Italian language oyster.

"Good morning," I sang out, feeling all the tension and worry of the last months dissipate in the face of this new job, the perfect job for this time of my life.

Judith looked at me, and her face paled. "Sadie. You're, *ehm,* here."

"Of course I'm here," I said. My smile spread to the others in the room when I realized they were watching us with interest. "I got your e-mail and found the place with no problem." I pulled up a chair from the perimeter and scooted it in between Judith and the blonde. "When do we start?" I asked, my voice hushed to encourage all the silent people to go back to their own conversations.

The dark-haired woman sitting next to Judith snickered and then put a hand over her mouth.

"Sadie," Judith said carefully, "I'm not sure what e-mail you're referring to."

"The one you sent about a month back. The preliminary schedule for the *Pasione* gig." I took a sharp breath. "Oh, no. Did I read it wrong? Is this meeting for something else? Like support staff? Chorus singers?"

The blonde sat back in her chair and smirked. Honestly, these people were starting to annoy me.

Judith pushed back her chair. "Sadie, can I see you out in the hall?"

I felt my heart drop to my stomach. "Of course," I said, following her out of the room and trying to ignore the flock of stares and giggles that accompanied me.

"What's going on?" I demanded once the door was closed. "Who are those people and what is their problem?"

"Sadie, I don't know how this got miscommunicated, but you have not been asked to be a part of *Pasione.*"

"What?" I sputtered. "But you said—"

Judith shook her head. "In the very, very early stages, I inquired about you as a possibility. But the producers were looking for something different. New talent, up-and-coming, fresh faces. You were just too ..." she searched for the word, "old establishment."

"Old establishment?" I shrieked. "I'm only forty years old!" My hand felt for the wall near me and I leaned on it for support.

"I know, I know." Judith's voice took on the well-practiced tone of a woman who knows how to placate people. "It's entirely unfair. But it's a business decision and they have their ticket sales to consider."

"But I moved back to New York ..." I trailed off. My head was spinning and I worried I might be sick.

"Listen, there will be other things." Judith peeked in the window on the door of the conference room. "I have some calls in to area churches for their spring concert series. And we can try to rebuild your opera presence through some smaller venues."

I concentrated on breathing in, breathing out.

"I'll call you," she said. She leaned over to kiss me on both cheeks. I didn't even bother reciprocating. "So sorry about the confusion." She heaved open the door and I caught a glimpse of a few snickering children before the door slammed behind her.

"Sadie, honey, pick up the phone."

Richard's voice on the answering machine cut through my fog and I tried in vain to open one eye.

"Sadie, pick up, babe. I've tried your cell and it goes

to voice mail. I know you're home and avoiding me. Pick up."

I flopped over to my other side and pulled the covers more tightly around my chin. Still he prattled on.

"That's it. I'm coming over. Pick up, or I'm coming over."

I could feel my numbed head slipping back toward sleep.

"This is your last chance," I heard through the blankets that draped over my ear, right before I spiraled downward once more into a colorless dream.

When I opened my eyes again, the room was washed in the ochre of an early summer evening. After a moment of gathering my thoughts to my room … my building, twelfth floor … Upper West Side … Manhattan, I realized someone or something was pounding on the apartment door.

"Sadie, open this blasted thing!" Panic poured out of Richard's voice and under my covers. I pushed myself up and willed my legs over the side of the bed. My socks padded over the tile in the entry way and my hands protested the sudden need for strength as I fumbled with the locks on the door.

"Oh, thank *God*," Richard exhaled when I opened the door. He threw himself into my arms, which were in no condition to be catching a melodramatic ex-husband. "I thought you'd given up." He sniffled into my hair. "The Brooklyn Bridge, the tracks of the A train, Empire State."

I pulled away and stared at him. "What are you talking about?"

"Suicide!" he said, exasperated at my daftness. "I thought you just couldn't take it anymore."

"So you've heard," I said. I pulled away from his sloppy embrace and shuffled to the kitchen. I lifted my teapot from the stove and let it fall to my side as I dragged it and my body to the sink.

Richard perched on one of the barstools on the other side of the counter. "Roxanne at the Met called me. I'm so sorry, sweetheart."

I looked up at him from the gushing faucet. "Roxanne at the Met? How did she know?"

He shrugged. "I don't know. Judith? Mary? Steven Michaels is the artistic director of *Pasione* and he's an old friend of Roxanne's husband."

I slammed down the faucet handle. "Fantastic. Mr. Roxanne, whoever he is, knows I am once again snubbed for a good role. Perhaps I should just get it over with and rent an ad in the *Times* declaring myself a formerly successful singer in search of work." I banged the teapot down on the burner and flipped on the gas flame. "But beware, I would say. I'm one heck of a liability, now that I'm forty. I fire my agents on a whim, I've lived in Iowa, *and* I'm part of the 'old establishment.'" I made violent quotation marks with my fingers as I spoke.

"Darling, calm down." Richard bit his lower lip and glanced at the teapot warming on the stove. "Your tea will be ready soon and we'll just sit and have a chat."

"I don't *want* to sit and have a chat." The emotional fatigue from the last few months collapsed within me and reformed into a wild, frustrated volcano. "I'm tired of chatting. I want to have people like my singing again, dang it!"

"We do, we do," Richard said, coming around the counter. He came to put an arm around me where I stood glaring at the teapot. "We do love your singing."

"Who loves my singing?" I furrowed my brow in a pout.

"I do, for one," Richard turned me toward him and I put my head on his shoulder. "A legion of loyal fans. Scores of musicians. Judith."

"Judith betrayed me," I said into his shirt.

"Are you sure?"

"No, but she could have returned my calls." I felt tears sting my eyes when I pictured again the smug looks on the faces in the conference room.

"She could have and she should have," Richard said and then sighed dramatically. "At least we always have each other."

I studied his face and felt my pulse quicken. "Not really."

His smile drooped. "Pardon?"

"We don't really have each other, do we, Richard?" I asked softly. "We tried once, it didn't work, and I think I've been putting everything on hold since then."

"What are you talking about?" he said, worried. "We date other people."

"No, *you* date other people. Adolescents. Whatever. But I don't. I've defined myself as what I do, rather than whom I love, the family I create. And you, Richard, are my only family."

"Is that so bad?" His tone was injured.

"It wouldn't be if we were still a couple."

"You want to get back together?" Fear streaked across his face.

"Good gracious, no," I laughed and he relaxed. "No need to repeat bad history." I looked away and shook my head. "He was right," I said quietly.

"Who was right?"

"Mac."

Richard paused and then, "Mac the pickup truck man?"

I nodded.

"Right about what?" he asked.

I shifted my gaze back to Richard. "Lots of things. But one of them was that I need to move on. From this." I gestured from myself to Richard.

He leaned back on the counter and shook his head. "I think Iowa screwed you up. No," he said, thinking twice, "I think it started even earlier. It was the John the Baptist Christmas Eve, wasn't it?" He nodded knowingly. "You've been loopy ever since."

I thought a moment. "You might be right. John did have an effect on me, though I think I'm just now starting to figure it out." I stepped forward and hugged my dear, sweet, narcissistic but endearing ex-husband. "We've been good friends, in our own, self-absorbed, needy ways."

He snickered into my hair.

I pulled back. "And I'll always love you for your many, many years of friendship, thick and thin. But," I took a deep breath and exhaled. The corners of my mouth curved upward and I said, "I think it's time for act two."

♪

That night, I sat on my bed, my room lit only by two muted bedside lamps. I held in my hands the small, leather-bound Bible Jayne had sneaked into one of my suitcases the day I'd jumped ship to the hotel. I'd left it in the outside pocket of that bag until this very moment. I opened the cover carefully, as if nervous that John the Baptist himself would come barreling out if I moved too quickly. The smell of new pages lifted up from the book. I ran one hand slowly down the title page. On the inside of the cover, Jayne's handwriting bore a blessing.

> "For I know the plans I have for you," declares the LORD, "plans to prosper you and not to harm you, plans to give you hope and a future. Then you will call upon me and come and pray to me, and I will listen to you. You will seek me and find me when you seek me with all your heart." Jeremiah 29:11–13.

I shut the book and held it to my chest. After a cascade of minutes spent staring out the window by the bed, I let myself fall onto the pillows and blankets, still clutching the book to me, still clinging to hope.

28

Curtain Call

The sun had set by the time we pulled up. A gradual wash of dark blue to pale yellow stretched from one horizon to the other, exuberant purples, reds, and oranges playing in between. I held a twenty over the front seat.

"Thanks, Tom. Keep the change."

His eyes widened slightly and he nodded. "Thank you." The door creaked as he leaped out to retrieve my small suitcase from the trunk. He rolled it carefully over to where I stood, eyes trained on the flowered front porch in the distance.

"You in town for long?" Tom asked softly. It was the longest sentence I'd ever heard from him.

"Hmm." I looked at the sky, pondering the weight

of that question. I turned my gaze to Maplewood's only cab driver. "I'll let you know." I smiled at the knowing look on Tom's face as he walked back quickly to his side, tipped his cap, and coaxed the station wagon into a slow lumber back down the highway.

I started down the long driveway toward the house and hoped those plans to prosper and not to harm me were just about ready to kick in.

I left my bag at the foot of the porch stairs and tiptoed up. The house was darkening right along with the sky and I wondered if I'd have to wait on the swing. I knocked softly on the front door. Through the open windows I could hear strains of music lilting out to the front yard. After another round of knocking, louder this time, I tried the doorknob and wasn't one bit surprised to find the door unlocked. I let myself in.

The music seemed to be coming from the kitchen, which was near the back of the house. I walked through the living room, past the oak staircase, down a short hallway and into the kitchen. The room faced west and so still enjoyed the warm light of a sun not yet set. My voice filled the air from the speakers of a Bose on the counter. A stack of Sadie Maddox CDs sat on the counter, recently opened by the looks of the cellophane wrappers littering the space in front of the stereo. The speakers pointed out a gaping window, my voice carrying Copland's "Simple Gifts" out of the house and into the open air.

The kitchen door led to a brick patio surrounded by more of the lush green and Technicolor planted on the front porch. Mac sat in a teak patio chair, ball cap on and arms folded, his legs stretched in front of him and crossed at the ankles. He sat with his back to the window, looking down into the small valley that yawned behind his home.

I closed my eyes and took a deep breath before pushing open the screen door.

Mac looked up.

I stood near the door, waiting for his reaction.

"Hi," he said. I thought I saw a softness in his eyes before he clenched his jaw and looked back toward the valley. "I was just thinking about you."

"Oh, dear." I walked slowly toward him and gestured toward an empty patio chair sitting next to him. "May I?"

Mac nodded. "Of course."

We sat without speaking, watching the greens deepen as the sun dipped below the trees.

"Nice music," I said, nodding toward the open window.

"Like that?" he said. A twinge of mischief in his voice made me relax a little. "I got them on deep discount."

"You get what you pay for." I allowed myself a small smile. "What happened to 'I Like My Women a Little on the Trashy Side'?"

He grinned, though still not in my direction. "Still got it. I can put it in after this, if you'd like."

"I'll keep that in mind." I realized I was worrying my watch and bracelet with my fingers. "Mac," I said, turning to him. "I'm so sorry."

He turned to look at me.

I cleared my throat. "I was wrong about quite a few

things and I think I hurt you." I searched his eyes. "Did I?"

He nodded slowly. "You did."

I kept his gaze. "I've spent my entire life working really hard to keep myself at the center of the universe. Turns out, it's not as good an idea as it once seemed."

Mac cocked his head to one side. "Go on."

"Listen," I said, suddenly impatient. "The crux of it is I read the Bible." I tried really hard not making those last two words sound like I was rolling my eyes, but Mac laughed anyway.

"Did you, now? And what did *the Bible* have to say that you found interesting?"

"Well, I found this part where God is saying that He has a plan for me. A good plan. And that if I seek Him, He'll let me in on it." I shrugged. "My plans haven't been going so well, so I think I'll give Him a turn."

Mac nodded, taking in every word as if he'd said these very things before.

I sighed. "I guess it just rang true. Like the homeless John the Baptist."

Mac's forehead wrinkled. "You met John the Baptist?"

I nodded. "I'm telling you. You can see *anything* in New York."

He shook his head at life in the Big Apple.

I continued. "It rings true like Jayne and her reaction to Handel, like a great sermon I heard, even though it came from a questionable messenger. And you." I turned to him, a lump forming in my throat. "You, Mac Hartley, ring true."

He smiled. "Can I gloat?"

I arched an eyebrow. "Not unless you want me to speed dial Tom for a quick cab ride back to the airport."

Mac stood from his chair and my heart jumped. He walked over to me and offered me a hand. I stood up and he wrapped his arms around my waist. I gave up trying to look composed and let my eyes fill with tears.

He leaned down to kiss me on the cheek, intersecting with a salty tear rolling down my face. "What's the first step of the plan?" he asked softly.

"I've been offered a year-long position at Moravia," I whispered, willing him not to move an inch.

"Way out here in the sticks?" he said, brushing another kiss, this time on my forehead.

"*Mm-hmm*," I said, eyes open and watching his take me in. "You people could use some high culture."

He nodded, kissed me on the other cheek. "This will never work, you know."

I traced one finger slowly down his cheek. "I know," I said with all seriousness. "You'd better work on a Plan B."

"Isn't that what this is?"

I let him gather me to him, my face on his chest, smelling the clean scent of his hair and skin. Behind us, the sun glittered on the horizon, turning the world all shades of light and dark, readying itself for the advent of a new day.

… a little more …

When a delightful concert comes to an end,
the orchestra might offer an encore.
When a fine meal comes to an end,
it's always nice to savor a bit of dessert.
When a great story comes to an end,
we think you may want to linger.
And so, we offer …

AfterWords—just a little something more after you
have finished a David C. Cook novel.
We invite you to stay awhile in the story.
Thanks for reading!

Turn the page for …

• An excerpt from *Stretch Marks,*
the new novel by Kimberly Stuart

When a daughter becomes a mother,
can she learn to accept her own?

Stretch Marks

a novel

Available fall 2009

13
Hail Mary
(text not final)

She forced herself to unwrap slowly from her zip-up sweatshirt. Bending down to untie her shoes, she needed to adjust for the belly that pressed down on her legs. She'd begun to feel the flutterings of a kicker within her womb, though she was never quite sure if she imagined movement or if she was experiencing the first steps toward communication with her child. It seemed fitting that the baby would start a maternal relationship with kicks and jabs. She often felt the desire to perform such catharsis with her own mother.

She walked slowly down the hall to the bathroom, clutching the letter in her hand. Lowering herself to the plush black rug in front of the sink, she carefully slit the envelope from one back corner to the other. He'd written on yellow legal paper, the way he began every piece of writing he did for hire.

Dear Mia,
I'm not exactly sure how to begin
a letter like this. Perhaps an apology is
the best way, the only way to start.
I'm sorry.

> The emptiness of those words
> must resound even more loudly where
> you are, but I offer them anyway as a
> necessary point of departure.

Mia heard a creak from the front hall and the sound of her mother taking off her coat. She reached over to shut the bathroom door and turned on the shower.

> I write to you from Seattle, which
> is sufficiently far away to feel I've
> removed myself from you and our
> "situation," but not far enough to feel
> very good about it.

Mia felt a wash of anger that their child had been reduced to a word within smug quotation marks, but she couldn't stop herself from reading on.

> I understand if you think I'm a
> coward and unworthy of contacting
> you after the way I reacted to your
> news. You're right. I showed nothing of
> bravery. Even now, I'm hiding behind
> my cowardice by writing instead of
> calling.

Or how about a visit, Mia thought wryly. *A visit would be appropriate.*

> But I'm hoping you'll recognize
> this small step I'm taking and allow me

> to begin a conversation with you once
> more. I'm feeling very overwhelmed,
> Mia, and very scared. This is not what
> I'd planned for our lives, certainly not
> now, and I'm having difficulty figuring
> out how I should respond.

Mia brushed off a tear that landed on the paper and smudged the black ink.

> I'll call soon. Or you can call me,
> if you'd prefer. I just want to talk.
> Maybe we can figure this mess out,
> the two of us. We always were pretty
> good together.
>
> Love, Lars

She sat with her legs splayed in front of her, the purple stripes on her yoga top muddied with tears. The spray from the shower drifted over the toilet, the sink, the floor, and her hair but Mia didn't get up to pull the curtain. He was ruining it, she thought. One letter, one look at his penmanship, his awkward sharing of his thoughts, reminders of the intimacy they'd earned after so many years. The defenses she'd carefully constructed over the months he'd been gone were crumbling at their foundations, even as she scurried around trying to keep them upright. *He's a jerk,* she said with authority to herself. *So what if he's a familiar one?*

She stayed there weeping until her eyes began to feel uncomfortably puffy and Babs knocked at the door.

"Mia?" she called. "Are you all right in there?"

Mia blew her nose into a wad of toilet paper.

"Honey? Can you hear me?" Worry had crept into Babs's tone. "You've been in there a very long time. I thought you were concerned about water conservation."

Mia reached up to turn the doorknob. She looked up at Babs through a fresh onslaught of tears. "Lars was the one worried about water conservation. I'm worried about the energy crisis." Her final words erupted into a wail and Babs dropped to her knees to gather her daughter into an embrace.

"Oh, honey, what's wrong? Are you feeling blue? Is it your figure? Sweetheart, you don't need to worry one bit. All those curves will go back to the right places after the baby's born."

Mia cried into her mother's shirt.

"Now, you'll need to be patient with yourself," Babs continued. "It takes nine months to grow a baby and it will take at least nine months to go back down to your regular size. Even then, you might have to think about surgery."

Mia shook her head and showed Babs the letter. "Lars wrote. He wants to start talking again."

Babs stared at the yellow paper. Her eyebrows knitted together and she lifted her gaze to Mia. "Is that a good thing or a despicable thing?" She spoke carefully and watched her daughter's face for a reaction.

Mia's mouth lifted into a shaky smile. "That's the question, isn't it?" She shook her head, grateful for her mother's uncharacteristic restraint. "I don't know yet."

Babs nodded slowly. "Honey, I don't know a lot about a lot of things, but I do know matters of the heart are more like a minefield and less like a Hallmark card, no matter what the songs say." She rose from her knees, creaking and moaning with every pop. "I'm old, Mia. I'm getting old."

Mia laughed and reached for another bunch of tissues as her mother turned off the shower.

"Listen," Babs said. She pulled Mia to her feet and cupped her swollen face between her hands. "I'm not one for mush, but this has to be said." She furrowed her brow in concentration as she looked into her daughter's eyes. "You are a beautiful, talented, smart woman with a big, big heart. You got the best of both of your parents and none of our flaws, which is nothing short of a miracle, considering we both had our share." Babs swallowed hard as Mia's eyes welled once more with tears. "You're going to give yourself time to figure out how to respond to this letter. I'll help you if I can, but I'm not sure I'm your best resource when it comes to man advice. Better ask Frankie. Or that nice girl from your high school graduating class—what was her name? Tiffany? Brittany?"

"Lindsay. Lindsay Dunlop."

"Right. She married very well, I hear, and could have some pointers."

Mia sighed and blotted her eyes with Kleenex.

"But before I forget, your obstetrician's office called while you were in the shower. Or on the bathroom floor getting misted."

"What did they say?"

"They called to confirm your ultrasound appointment for Wednesday at three." Babs's eyes lit up like candles. "May I come? Please? Please, Mia?"

"Come to my appointment?" Mia clutched her head, which had begun to pound with a new flush of hormones in the aftermath of emotion. "I suppose so. If you really want to and have no other plans."

"I'd thought about taking that lovely river cruise, the one about architecture? And I have a mani-pedi appointment at noon, but I can do both of those any day." Babs clapped her hands together. "Oh, thank you. I'm so, so excited. This is the fun part. And don't worry. I'll be quiet as a mouse. You won't even know I'm there unless you *summon* me." She smiled at Mia and pulled an arm around her waist as she ushered her to the living room. "Now, you sit down and I'll get you a few squares of dark chocolate. Nature's best mood lifters."

Mia watched Babs swish from the room and allowed a tiny crack to form in her protective wall.

✳ ✳ ✳

The next morning was a Sunday and Mia made a special effort to snuggle deeper inside her covers to take advantage of a late morning's sleep. Her eyes were still slightly swollen from the weeping-shower experience the day before, so when she woke at nine unable to drift back to sleep, the heaviness in her eyelids disoriented her into thinking it was much earlier than it was. She pulled on a bathrobe and shuffled in slippers to the kitchen.

"Good morning," Babs said as she beat Mia to the cupboard to retrieve a tea mug.

"You're awfully chipper," Mia said in a man-voice,

any unexpected affection for her mother from the day before evaporating in the merciless clarity of morning. "Why are you all dressed up?"

"These old rags?" Babs waved a bored hand across her red pencil skirt, white and red floral silk blouse, and four-inch heels. "Just something I dug up from the bottom of my bag."

Mia raised one weary eyebrow in her mother's direction.

"And ironed," Babs added. She handed her daughter a steaming cup of tea.

Mia sloshed a bit of cream into the cup and swirled the liquid into a lazy tornado. "Where are you headed?"

"I thought I'd go to church." Babs's back was turned to Mia as she rinsed her breakfast dishes in the sink. "Our services on the ship are usually very disappointing. We have to accommodate all preferences, but usually the Methodists win out. Very opinionated, those Methodists. I've sung many ancient hymns on the deep waters of the Caribbean."

Mia sipped her tea while leaning one hip against the counter. "I didn't know you were still a churchgoer."

Babs shrugged slightly. "I've never been as consistent as my parents would have liked. But there's nothing like the birth of one's first grandbaby to get one to the altar, as it were. This baby will need to baptized, you know." She wavered at the look on her daughter's face. "Just a little sprinkle?"

Mia shook her head. "I haven't decided on any of that. But as for this morning, there are a million churches in Chicago. I'm sure you'll find one that suits you." She sat down at the kitchen table and opened the newspaper.

"We can go wherever you want," Babs said. She swirled water and soap inside a glass before dumping it out. "I thought we could leave in a half hour or so and start wandering. Surely there's a good ten-thirty or eleven o'clock service close by."

Mia smirked over her cup. "Thanks for the invitation, Mother, but I'm no longer required to go to church with you. Adulthood exempts me from the guilt."

Babs looked injured. "Well, I can't force you." She was quiet for a moment. "But it would be some nice mother-daughter time. And I'll take you to lunch afterwards."

Mia could feel the weight of this decades-long argument settle with a familiar thud in her chest. "I don't think—"

"I know, I know," Babs said quickly. "The church has been used as an instrument of torture, it spreads propaganda that has nothing to do with the peace-loving granola Jesus of the Bible, it suppresses the rights of the women and the cause of the poor, and so on and so forth." She wiped her hands on a kitchen towel and looked up at Mia. "I've heard you."

"Great," Mia shrugged. "So we don't have to have this conversation again. You are free to attend church as consistently or inconsistently as you'd like and I'm free to do the same." She turned back to the paper.

"But the church *does* do lots of good things like weddings and funerals. And soup kitchens! You love soup kitchens! Besides, you might just need their help one day, miss, and this is a perfect time to look for a place to start building relationships. I met your father at church, you'll remember." She wagged her finger at her daughter.

"And look how well that turned out," Mia said. She rose to dump the dregs of her tea into the sink.

"Well," Babs said, not a bit flustered by the mention of her failed marriage, "you can't blame the church for that. We'd stopped going by that time, anyway." She stopped Mia on her way out of the kitchen. "Mimi, please. It won't hurt you. And I won't bother you about it for the rest of my visit."

Mia wavered. She rubbed her eyes with one hand.

Babs saw the weakening of resolve and jumped in to the silence. "After all, you're in good company, being knocked up with no husband. Think of the Virgin Mary!" She smiled in triumph.

Mia shook her head. "It is amazing I am so well-adjusted," she muttered as she walked to the bathroom.

"Great! I'll just pop downstairs and ask Sam about neighborhood churches."

Mia leaned her head against the tile as she waited for the water to warm. *The Virgin Mary, eh?* she thought. *Not exactly an airtight comparison.* She slipped into the shower and tried to prepare herself for a very long Sabbath.